William Shakespeare's The Merchant of Venice: A Retelling in Prose

David Bruce

Published by David Bruce, 2022.

This is a work of fiction. Similarities to real people, places, or events are entirely coincidental.

WILLIAM SHAKESPEARE'S THE MERCHANT OF VENICE: A RETELLING IN PROSE

First edition. July 27, 2022.

Copyright © 2022 David Bruce.

ISBN: 979-8201580179

Written by David Bruce.

Table of Contents

Dedication

Dedicated to My Sister Brenda

Brenda wrote, "During COVID and when visitors were restricted from visiting their loved one in the assisted-living facility I worked at, a patient mentioned to me how much she liked spaghetti during a late-night conversation we had. She was a night owl like me. Her name was Dee. I called her "Gerdy." Then she would say, "Dirty Gerdy," and we'd laugh. Anyway, on my way to work I bought two spaghetti meals from Olive Garden. I left for work early that night. I went to work, set up outlet dinners in the dining room, went to her room and wheeled her down to the dining room where we had dinner together. At that time, the residents weren't leaving their room and had their meals alone in their room. It was nighttime and everyone was already in bed, so I didn't see a problem. She was so grateful and had enough food for three more meals. It was such a simple gesture, but during that time it meant so much to her and for me."

Brenda once bought a newspaper at a gas station on Thanksgiving and tipped the female employee $5, and the employee cried.

Brenda wrote, "I do remember that. I also remember when George tipped a TeeJays waitress $100, and she cried. Our family does a lot of good deeds all the time: I unload people's grocery carts when the people are in those electric scooters. If they are alone with a few groceries, I'll leave cash for the cashier to pay for the groceries. I've had a lot of good deeds done to me when I didn't have a lot of money. It feels good to pay it forward."

She added, "I just have one more thing to add and then I'm done. I've had a lot of people in my life do good deeds for me when I was at a low point on my life. I was at a low point for a very long time. David, you know what you've done for me, and I can never thank you enough. Martha paid for antibiotics for me when I had strep throat and didn't have money. Rosa bought me groceries. Carla has done so much, and she had us over for Easter just after Chad died. When I say US, I mean all of my kids. She was so sick and ended up at the Emergency Room that same night. Frank gave me a car. And George buys my gas for me whenever he's in Florida. And Mom and Dad were good people. I had a lot of good influences in my life that made me be a good person. At least I hope I'm a good person. I try to be someone Mom and Dad would be proud of."

***

The doing of good deeds is important. As a free person, you can choose to live your life as a good person or as a bad person. To be a good person, do good deeds. To be a bad person, do bad deeds. If you do good deeds, you will become good. If you do bad deeds, you will become bad. To become the person you want to be, act as if you already are that kind of person. Each of us chooses what kind of person we will become. To become a good person, do the things a good person does. To become a bad person, do the things a bad person does. The opportunity to take action to become the kind of person you want to be is yours.

Cover Illustration for William Shakespeare's *The Merchant of Venice*: A Retelling in Prose
Illustration from *Tales from Shakespeare*, 1901.

Educate Yourself
Read Like A Wolf Eats
Be Excellent to Each Other
Books Then, Books Now, Books Forever

***

In this retelling, as in all my retellings, I have tried to make the work of literature accessible to modern readers who may lack some of the knowledge about mythology, religion, and history that the literary work's contemporary audience had.

Do you know a language other than English? If you do, I give you permission to translate this book, copyright your translation, publish or self-publish it, and keep all the royalties for yourself. (Do give me credit, of course, for the original retelling.)

I would like to see my retellings of classic literature used in schools, so I give permission to the country of Finland (and all other countries) to give copies of this book to all students forever. I also give permission to the state of Texas (and all other states) to give copies of this book to all students forever. I also give permission to all teachers to give copies of this book to all students forever.

Teachers need not actually teach my retellings. Teachers are welcome to give students copies of my eBooks as background material. For example, if they are teaching Homer's *Iliad* and *Odyssey*, teachers are welcome to give students copies of my *Virgil's* Aeneid: *A Retelling in Prose* and tell students, "Here's another ancient epic you may want to read in your spare time."

CAST OF CHARACTERS

Male Characters

DUKE OF VENICE.

PRINCE OF MOROCCO & PRINCE OF ARRAGON, Suitors to Portia.

ANTONIO, a Merchant of Venice.

BASSANIO, his Friend.

GRATIANO, SOLANIO, & SALARINO: Friends to Antonio and Bassanio.

LORENZO, in love with Jessica, Shylock's daughter.

SHYLOCK, a rich Jew.

TUBAL, a Jew, Shylock's friend.

LAUNCELOT GOBBO, a Clown, Servant first to Shylock and then to Bassanio.

OLD GOBBO, Father to Launcelot.

LEONARDO, Servant to Bassanio.

SALERIO, a Messenger from Venice and Gratiano's friend.

BALTHAZAR & STEPHANO: Servants to Portia.

Female Characters

PORTIA, a rich Heiress.

NERISSA, her waiting-woman. Nerissa is a gentlewoman; her social status is high enough that she can marry a gentleman.

JESSICA, Daughter to Shylock.

Minor Characters

Magnificoes of Venice, Officers of the Court of Justice, Jailer, Servants to Portia, and other Attendants.

Scene

Partly at Venice, Italy, the home of Antonio and Bassanio, and partly at Belmont, Italy, the home of Portia.

CHAPTER 1

On a street in Venice, Antonio and his friends Salarino and Solanio were talking.

Antonio said, "Truly, I do not know why I am melancholy. It wearies me; you say it wearies you. But how I caught it, found it, or came by it, what stuff it is made of, whereof it is born, I do not know. Melancholy makes me such an idiot — such a want-wit — that I have much trouble to know myself."

Salarino knew that Antonio had many merchant ships currently on the sea, and so he thought that Antonio must be worried about them.

Salarino said, "Your mind is tossing on the ocean. That is where your argosies — your large merchant ships — with their stately sails, as if they were signiors and rich burghers — gentlemen and prosperous freemen — are. They are like great floats in parades — the pageants of the sea. Your ships are so large that they look down on the petty traffickers, small ships that curtsy to them by lowering their flags to show them respect as they fly by with their woven wings."

Solanio said, "Believe me, sir, had I such risky ventures going forth on the seas, the better part of my concerns would be about my hopes abroad. I would always be plucking a blade of grass and dropping it to find out in what direction the wind is blowing. I would always be peering at maps looking for ports and piers and anchorages. Everything that might make me fear that my risky ventures would not be successful would, no doubt, make me melancholy."

Solanio said, "I would always be imagining harm coming to my ships at sea. Whenever I blew my breath over my soup to cool it, I would go into a fit of trembling because I would think what harm a too-great wind at sea could do to my ships. Whenever I would see the sand in an hourglass fall from the top to the bottom, I would think of shallows and of sandbars and I would see my wealth-bearing ship *Andrew* docked in sand and not in a safe port. I would see the high top of the main mast of my *Andrew* fall lower than her ribs — her wooden sides — and kiss her burial-ground. Whenever I went to church and saw the holy edifice of stone, I would immediately think of dangerous rocks, which by touching my noble vessel's side, would scatter all her cargo of valuable spices on the ocean stream and clothe the roaring waters with my cargo of silk cloth. In short, I would always be thinking that at one moment I would own a valuable cargo, but in the next moment, due to misfortunes at sea, I would own nothing. Would I be able to think about these things and not become melancholy? No, of course not. No one needs to tell me why Antonio is melancholy. He is worried about his ships and their cargos of merchandise."

"Believe me, I am not worried about my business ventures at sea," Antonio said. "I thank my fortune — both my wealth and my luck — that I am not worried about such misfortunes as you think I am. I am a good businessman; I am diversified. I am not risking everything in a single ship. I am not risking everything in trading with a single country. Unless exceedingly great misfortunes happen, I will not go bankrupt anytime soon and certainly not this year. Therefore, my business ventures at sea are not making me melancholy."

"Why, then you are in love," Salarino said.

"Hardly," Antonio replied.

"So you are not in love, either?" Salarino said. "In that case, we may as well say that you are sad because you are not merry. Saying that is as easy as saying that you laugh and leap and are merry because you are not sad. Now, by the god Janus, who has one head but two faces that look in different directions, Nature has created some strange fellows in her time. Some fellows are always happy: They have to peep through their eye-slits because their eyes are always half-closed due to constant laughter; they laugh like happy parrots at a melancholy bagpiper and at others who look as if they have been drinking vinegar and would never laugh and show their teeth during a laugh even if Nestor, the wise and old and serious advisor of the Greek army at Troy, thought that a jest was worth laughing at."

Bassanio, Lorenzo, and Gratiano now came walking toward them. All three were Antonio's friends, but Bassanio was Antonio's best friend.

"Here comes Bassanio, your most noble kinsman," Solanio said. "Here also come Gratiano and Lorenzo. Fare you well. We leave you now with better company."

"I would have stayed until I had made you merry," Salarino said, "but now worthier friends than I can do that."

"I regard your friendship as very dear and I know that your businesses are important," Antonio said. "I understand why you need to leave. Your own businesses call on you, and now you embrace this occasion — the arrival of other friends — to depart."

"Good morning, my good lords," Salarino said.

"Good signiors both, when shall we meet together and have fun? Say, when?" Bassanio said. "You grow exceedingly strange and distant. Must you be so?"

"We will arrange our leisures to attend on yours," Salarino said. "We will find time to get together with you."

Salarino and Solanio departed.

Lorenzo said, "My Lord Bassanio, since you have found Antonio, we two will leave you, but please remember that we will meet at dinnertime."

"I will remember," Bassanio said.

"You do not look well, Signior Antonio," Gratiano said. "You think too seriously about worldly affairs. If you worry too much, you will lose the ability to enjoy yourself. Believe me, you are marvelously changed."

"I regard the world as only the world, Gratiano," Antonio replied. "It is a stage on which every man must play a part, and my part is a melancholy one."

"Let me play the fool," Gratiano said. "With mirth and laughter let old wrinkles — laugh lines — come. I prefer for my body to be heated with wine rather than cooled with mortifying groans. Why should a man, whose blood is warm inside his veins, sit like his dead grandsire's alabaster statue? Why should a man seem to be asleep when he is awake? Why should a man cause himself to become ill by being peevish? Let me tell you, Antonio, I respect you, and it is out of my friendship that I say this: There is a sort of men whose pale faces are like a pond covered with algae. Such men cultivate an obstinate silence because they want to win a reputation for being possessed of wisdom, gravity, and profound thought. It is as if they want to be able to say, 'I am Sir Oracle, and when I open my lips let no dog bark!' They are aware that oracles are supposed to speak for a god and that dogs are thought to bark at people who are in disgrace. Antonio, I know men who are thought to be wise only because they say nothing, but I am very sure that if these men would ever speak, other people would dam their ears by putting their fingers in them to stop them from hearing nonsense. They would also damn their ears because when they heard such nonsense they would call these brothers fools and so run afoul of Matthew 5:22: *'But I say unto you, That whosoever is angry with his brother without a cause shall be in danger of the judgment: and whosoever shall say to his brother, Raca [an insulting term], shall be in danger of the council: but whosoever shall say, Thou fool, shall be in danger of hell fire.'* I will tell you more about this another time. So do not fish for a reputation for wisdom by using your melancholy as bait. Reputation can be worthless and not based on reality."

Gratiano then said, "Come, good Lorenzo. It is time for us to go."

He said to Antonio, "Farewell for a while. I'll end my exhortation after dinner. I am like a preacher who goes on far too long to finish his sermon before dinner and so must resume his sermon after dinner."

Lorenzo said to Antonio, "We will leave you then until dinner-time. Apparently, I must be one of these same dumb and never-speaking wise men because Gratiano speaks so much that he never lets me speak."

"Keep me company for two more years," Gratiano joked, "and you shall forget the sound of your own tongue."

"Farewell," Antonio said. "I will take your advice and become more talkative."

"Thank you," Gratiano said. "Truly, silence is only commendable in a dried beef tongue — or should I say an impotent old man — or in an adult virgin who is not marriageable — or should I say an old maid."

Gratiano and Lorenzo departed.

Antonio asked, "What was that all about?"

"Gratiano speaks an infinite deal about nothing, more than any man in all Venice," Bassanio said. "His ideas are like two grains of wheat hidden in two bushels of chaff: You shall seek all day before you find them, and when you have them, they are not worth the search."

"Well, tell me now which lady is it for whom you swore to make a secret pilgrimage," Antonio said. "You promised to tell me that today."

"It is not unknown to you, Antonio, how much I have squandered my estate by enjoying more prodigal and lavish living than my small means would allow me to continue. Nor do I now make moan and complain about being forced to stop such lavish living; instead, my chief concern is to extricate myself — honorably — from the great debts I have incurred by living so lavishly. To you, Antonio, I owe the most, both in money and in friendship. Because of your friendship to me, I feel able to tell you my plan for getting clear of the debts I owe."

"Please, good Bassanio, let me know your plan. If your plan is, as you yourself always are, honorable, be assured that my wallet, my person, and my resources will help you in your plan."

"During my schooldays," Bassanio said, "when I had shot and lost one arrow, I would shoot a similar arrow — one of the same weight and with the same pattern of feathers — in the same direction and with the same force that I had shot the first arrow. By risking the second arrow, I often found both it and the first arrow because I watched the second arrow more carefully than I had watched the first arrow. I am telling you about this childhood experience because it is relevant to what I am going to propose to you — my proposal is guileless like the proposal of a child. The money that I owe you is spent (by an impetuous youth) and gone, but if you please to shoot another arrow the same way that you shot the first arrow I do not doubt that I will be more careful and closely watch the second arrow and so find both arrows, or if not, I will find the second arrow and bring back to you the second amount of money I borrowed and thank you and continue to owe you the first amount of money I borrowed."

"You ought to know me well," Antonio said. "Right now you are wasting time by not speaking plainly; instead, you are circling around what you want to ask me to do. You doubt that I will help you, and by so doubting my friendship and my willingness to help you, you do more wrong than if you had wasted everything I have. Therefore, tell me plainly what you want me to do and what you know I am able to do. If you do so, I will do what you want me to do. Therefore, speak to me plainly."

"In the town of Belmont is a lady who has been made rich by inheritance. She is beautiful, and what is more beautiful than that beauty, she has wondrous virtues. Sometimes from her eyes I have received encouraging but speechless messages: She likes me. Her name is Portia, and she is in no way of lesser value than the Portia who was Cato's daughter and Brutus' wife — the Portia who was renowned for her devotion to her husband. Nor is the wide world ignorant of the worth of Portia of Belmont; the four winds blow in from every coast renowned suitors who wish to marry her. She has sunny locks of hair that hang on her temples like a golden fleece — that fleece that Jason sailed to Colchis in quest of. Now many Jasons come in quest of Portia. Antonio, if I had the means to be one of the men who travel to and seek to marry Portia, I truly believe — and my mind prophesies — that I would without question be the one who wins her! Therefore, I ask you to lend me money that will enable me to travel to Belmont and woo Portia."

"You know that all my fortune is invested in ships at sea," Antonio said. "I have neither the money you need nor merchandise that I can sell to raise the money you need. Therefore, go forth; see what my credit is worth in Venice. I will use all of my credit to raise the money you need — I will stretch my credit as far as it will stretch to get you the money you need to sail to Belmont and court beautiful Portia. Go, immediately inquire, and so will I, where money can be borrowed, and I believe without question that I can raise the money either from business loans or from loans from friends."

— 1.2 —

Portia and her waiting-gentlewoman, Nerissa, who was her companion and confidante, talked together in a room of Portia's house in Belmont.

"Truly, Nerissa, my little body is weary of this great world."

"You would be weary of this great world, sweet madam, if your miseries were as abundant as your good fortunes are. However, as far as I can see, people who stuff themselves with too much food are as sick as people who starve because they have no food. It is no mean — small — happiness, therefore, to be seated in the mean — middle. Those in the middle achieve Aristotle's golden mean and so do not eat too much or too little food and so avoid sickness. People who eat too much grow white hair and age quickly; people who eat the right amount of food live longer. People should try to achieve the golden mean and so be virtuous."

"Those are good moral maxims, and you have well delivered them," Portia said.

"They would be better moral maxims if people actually followed them."

"If to do the right thing were as easy as to know what the right thing to do is, small chapels would be large churches and the cottages of poor men would be the palaces of Princes. It is a good preacher who follows the instructions he gives in his own sermons. I can easier teach twenty people what things were good to be done, than be one of the twenty who would follow my own teaching. The brain may devise rules for controlling one's temper, but a hot temper leaps over a cold rule. Mad, passionate youth skips over the good counsel given by wisdom, that old cripple. A youth is like a hare that jumps over the nets that are supposed to ensnare it. But this kind of talk and this kind of

7

reasoning is not going to help me choose a husband. But I should not use the word 'choose.' I may neither choose whom I wish to marry nor refuse whom I do not wish to marry. And so the psychological will of a living daughter is curbed by the legal will of a dead father. Is it not hard, Nerissa, that I cannot choose a man to be a husband nor refuse a man who wins me to be his wife?"

"Your father was always virtuous; and holy men at their death have good inspirations. It is said that dying virtuous men have special insight and can foretell the future. Therefore, the lottery that your father devised on his deathbed is the right way to choose your future husband. Here before us lie three caskets or boxes. The first casket is made of gold, the second of silver, and the third of lead. Whichever suitor chooses the casket your father wants your future husband to choose will, no doubt, be exactly the man whom you ought to marry. But do you like any of these Princely suitors who have already come to court you?"

"Name them one by one, and as you name them, I will describe them. By listening to my description of each of them, you can determine which of them, if any, I like."

"First, there is the Neapolitan Prince — this Prince comes from Naples."

"Yes, and he is a colt indeed — he is an uncouth young man. He does nothing but talk about his horse, and he thinks that it is a great accomplishment and a credit to himself that he can shoe his own horse. I am very much afraid that his mother committed adultery with a blacksmith."

"Then there is the Count Palatine. This nobleman has supreme jurisdiction over his own county."

"He does nothing but frown, as if he were saying, 'If you will not have me, so be it — do as you please.' He hears merry tales and yet he does not smile, I fear he will prove to be a weeping philosopher when he grows old because he is so full of impolite and inappropriate seriousness in his youth. In his old age, he will be like Heraclitus, the philosopher who wept when he saw human stupidity. In his old age, he will not be like Democritus, the laughing philosopher who valued cheerfulness. I had rather be married to a death's-head — a skull — with a bone in his mouth than to either of these men. May God keep me away from these two men!"

"What do you think about Monsieur Le Bon, the French lord?"

"God made him, and therefore let us assume that he is a man," Portia replied. "Truly, I know it is a sin to be a mocker, but this man — why, he has a horse better than the Neapolitan's and a better bad habit of frowning than the Count Palatine! He imitates every man and therefore he is no man — he does not have an identity of his own. If a thrush begins to sing, he immediately begins to dance. He fences with his own shadow. If I were to marry him, it would be like marrying twenty husbands because he has no identity of his own. If he would despise me, I would forgive him because if he were to love me to madness, I would never be able to return his love."

"What do you say about Falconbridge, the young Baron from England?"

"You know I say nothing to him because he cannot understand me and I cannot understand him. He does not know Latin, French, or Italian, and you could come into a law court and accurately swear that I have a poor pennyworth's worth of knowledge of English. He is the picture of a proper man, but, alas, who can have a conversation with a picture or with a mime? And how oddly he dresses! I think he bought his jacket in Italy, his stockings in France, and his hat in Germany. His manners seem to come from everywhere."

"What do you think of the Scottish lord, his neighbor?"

"The Scottish lord must have a neighborly charity. The Englishman lent him a box on the ear, and the Scottish lord swore he would pay him again when he was able. I think that the Englishman must have also lent the Frenchman a box on the ear and that the Scottish lord and the Frenchman joined forces and swore to someday pay the Englishman back."

"How do you like the young German, the Duke of Saxony's nephew?"

"I like him very vilely in the morning, when he is sober, and most vilely in the afternoon, when he is drunk. When the German is at his best, he is little worse than a man, and when he is at his worst, he is little better than a beast. If the worst that could happen ever happened — I married him and he died — I'm pretty sure that I could manage to live my life without him."

"If he were to make the trial of the three caskets, and if he were to choose the right casket, you ought to refuse to perform your father's will — you ought to refuse to marry the young German."

"Therefore, for fear of the worst, please set a deep glass of white wine from the Rhineland on one of the wrong caskets because even if the Devil is within the casket he will choose the casket that has the alcoholic temptation on it —

I know he will choose it. I will do anything, Nerissa, before I'll be married to a sponge who sops up alcohol."

"You need not fear, lady, marrying any of these lords. They have told me what they have decided: They will return to their homes and not bother you by courting you unless they can do so without having to choose one of the three caskets."

"Whoever marries me must choose the right casket," Portia said. "If I live to be as old as the Sibyl, whom the god Apollo granted as many years of life as she was able to hold grains of sand in her hands, I will die as chaste as the virgin goddess Diana, unless I be obtained by the manner ordered in my father's will. I am glad that this parcel of wooers is so reasonable because there is not one among them whose absence I do not greatly desire, and I pray that God grants them a fair departure."

"Do you remember a Venetian who is a scholar and a soldier and who came hither in company of the Marquis of Montferrat while your father was still alive?" Nerissa asked.

"Yes, yes, he was Bassanio," Portia said. "I think that was his name."

She thought, *Bassanio was definitely his name, but I don't want Nerissa to know that I am interested in him.*

"Truly, madam, he, of all the men that ever my foolish eyes looked upon, was the man who best deserved a fair and beautiful lady to be his wife."

Pleased, Portia said, "I remember him well, and I remember him as being worthy of your praise."

An attendant entered the room.

Portia said to him, "How are you? What is the news you bring?"

The attendant replied, "The strangers who came here to court you, madam, have come here to say goodbye to you. In addition, a herald has come to announce that his master, the Prince of Morocco, will arrive here tonight to court you."

Portia replied, "If I could bid this new suitor welcome with as good a heart as I can bid my other suitors farewell, I would be glad that he is coming. But if the Prince of Morocco has the character of a saint and the black complexion of a Devil, I had rather that he shrive me than wive me — I had rather that he hear me confess than see me in a wedding dress. I confess that the skin color of my future husband is important to me, as is his character."

She added, "Come, Nerissa."

Then she said to the attendant, "Walk in front of us."

Finally, she joked, "While we shut the gates upon one wooer, another knocks at the door."

— 1.3 —

In a public place in Venice, Bassanio was meeting with Shylock to ask the Jew of Venice to lend him money with Antonio as the guarantor. In all, he wanted three thousand ducats, aka Venetian gold coins.

Shylock said, "Three thousand ducats. Well."

"Yes, sir, for three months."

"For three months. Well."

"For which, as I told you, Antonio shall be the guarantor. Antonio shall legally bind himself to pay back that money I borrow from you if I cannot pay it back."

"Antonio shall be the guarantor. Well."

"Will you supply me with the money? Will you oblige me? Can you tell me now either yes or no?"

Shylock said, "Three thousand ducats for three months and Antonio legally bound as guarantor."

"Yes. What is your answer: yes or no?"

"Antonio is a good man."

"Have you heard any imputation to the contrary?"

"Oh, no, no, no, no," Shylock said. "You mistake my meaning. When I said that he is a good man, I meant that he should be adequate security for the loan. Yet his wealth is at risk. He has one merchant ship bound for Tripolis and another bound for the Indies. I understand, moreover, from talking to people at the Rialto, the mercantile exchange here in Venice, that he has a third merchant ship bound for Mexico and a fourth one bound for England, and he has other business ventures scattered — and perhaps squandered — abroad. We must realize that ships are only boards and that sailors are only men. There exist land-rats and water-rats, water-thieves and land-thieves — I mean that pirates exist — and then there is the peril of waters, winds, and rocks. This man, Antonio, is, notwithstanding, good security for this loan. Three thousand ducats: I think I may make this loan with him as guarantor."

"You may be sure that you can."

"I will be assured that I can, and to ensure that I am sure, I will carefully think about making this loan. May I speak with Antonio?"

"If it will please you to dine with us."

"Dine with you? And to smell pork and to eat of the habitation that your prophet the Nazarite conjured the Devil into? In Mark 5:1-13 of your holy book, we read of the man who was possessed by demons. Jesus ordered the demons to leave the possessed man and to enter the bodies of some pigs that rushed down a steep bank and entered a lake and were drowned. Such food is not kosher, and I am an observant Jew. I will buy with you, sell with you, talk with you, walk with you, and so on, but I will not eat with you, drink with you, or pray with you. What news comes from the Rialto?"

Shylock looked up and added, "Who is that man who is coming here?"

Bassanio said, "He is Signior Antonio."

Shylock thought, *Antonio looks like a fawning publican. When I say "fawning," I am being sarcastic because he is proud and does not fawn, but despite his pride he will ask me to lend his friend money. But he is very much like a publican — a Roman tax collector. Like a publican, he will take from the Jews their profit and give it to his gentile masters. I hate Antonio because he is a Christian. But I hate him even more because in his humble foolishness he lends money without charging interest and so brings down the rate of interest we moneylenders can charge in Venice. If I get the advantage of him — if I were a wrestler, I would say, if I can catch him once upon the hip so that I can throw him to the ground — I will feed fat the ancient grudge I bear him and get a great revenge. Antonio hates our sacred nation, he hates us Jews, and he rails — even in the place where merchants most often do congregate — against me and against my business deals and well-won profit, which he calls undeserved interest. Cursed be my tribe of Jews if I forgive him!*

"Shylock, are you listening?" Bassanio asked.

"I am reckoning up how much ready money I have, and I think that I cannot immediately raise the full amount of three thousand ducats. But that does not matter. Tubal, a wealthy Hebrew of my tribe, will lend me the additional amount you need to borrow. But wait! For how many months do you need to borrow the money?"

Shylock said to Antonio, "I hope that you are well, good signior. We were just talking about you. Your name was the last name in our mouths."

Antonio replied, "Shylock, although I neither lend nor borrow with interest — paying it when I borrow or collecting it when I lend — yet, to help my friend get the money he urgently needs, I will break my custom."

He said to Bassanio, "Does Shylock know how much money you need?"

Shylock replied for Bassanio, "Yes, yes, three thousand ducats."

Antonio added, "And he needs it for three months."

Shylock said, "I had forgotten. Three months."

He said to Bassanio, "You did tell me that."

He added, "Well, then, we need a legal contract. Let me see. Antonio, I think that you said that you neither charge or pay interest."

"That is true."

Shylock said, "Jacob used to be the shepherd to his uncle Laban's sheep. This Jacob was descended from our holy Abraham. First came Abraham, then his son Isaac, and then his grandson Jacob in the line of Jewish patriarchs. Jacob's wise mother, Rebecca, helped him deceive Isaac so that Jacob and not his elder brother, Esau, would become Isaac's heir. This story is told in Genesis 27. Yes, Jacob was the third Jewish patriarch."

"What about him?" Antonio asked. "Did he charge interest?"

"He did not charge interest," Shylock said. "That is, he did not charge interest *directly*, as you would say. Listen as I tell you what he did. Laban and Jacob made an agreement that all the lambs that would be born with fleeces of two colors — for example, black and white — would be Jacob's payment for services rendered as shepherd. In the autumn, the ewes, being in heat, turned to the rams to be bred. Jacob, the skillful shepherd, took some branches and peeled away some of the bark so that the branches were dark where the bark was and light where the bark had been peeled away. These he set before the ewes as they were being bred because he believed that the ewes that saw the branches of two colors would give birth to lambs of two colors. And so it happened: The ewes gave birth to many lambs of two colors in the spring, and those lambs became the property of Jacob. Jacob thrived, and he was blest. Such thriving is a blessing, as long as men do not steal in order to thrive."

Antonio said, "Jacob had to work as a shepherd in order to thrive, and he had the help of God, Who made the lambs of two colors. This was not a thing that Jacob had the power to bring to pass — simply looking at partly peeled branches will not make a ewe give birth to lambs of two colors. All of that was governed and shaped by the hand of Heaven. Why did you tell us this story? Are you trying to justify charging interest on loans? That is a poor justification. Jacob worked hard for his profit, and one problem that people have with usury is that the usurer does no work. Also, sheep can breed, but metal coins cannot breed. Do you consider your gold and silver to be ewes and rams?"

"I don't know if my gold and silver can legitimately be compared to ewes and rams, but I do know that I make my gold and silver breed as fast as ewes and rams. But listen to me, Signior Antonio."

Antonio ignored Shylock and said, "Listen well, Bassanio. This is important. The Devil can cite Scripture for his purpose. An evil soul producing holy witness is like a villain who smiles from cheek to cheek. He is like an apple that appears to be good but is rotten at the heart. Falsehood can put on a good-seeming disguise."

Wanting to change the subject of conversation back to the loan, Shylock thought out loud, "Three thousand ducats: It is a good round sum. Three months from twelve; then, let me see, what will be the interest rate?"

Antonio asked, "Well, Shylock, will you lend us the money?"

Shylock replied, "Signior Antonio, many a time and often in the Rialto you have berated me about my moneylending and about my charging of interest. Always I have borne it with a patient shrug because patient forbearance is the mark of all our tribe of Jews. You call me a heretic and an unbeliever and a cutthroat dog, and you spit upon my Jewish garments, and you do that because I am making use of what I myself own. In your own holy book — Matthew 20:15 — is written, *Is it not lawful for me to do what I will with mine own?* Well, it now appears you need my help. Ha! You come to me, and you say 'Shylock, I want to borrow money.' You say this — you, who spat upon my beard and kicked me as you would kick a strange dog to get it out of your house. You need to borrow money. What should I say to you? Should I not say, 'Has a dog money? Is it possible a cur can lend three thousand ducats?' Or should I bow low and with a slave's voice anxiously and humbly whisper, 'Fair sir, you spit on me last Wednesday. You kicked me on a different day. On another day you called me a dog. Because you have shown me these courtesies, should I answer, 'Yes, I will lend you the money you need'?"

"I am likely to call you those names again, to spit on you again, and to kick you again," Antonio said. "If you will lend me this money, do not lend it as if you were lending it to a friend — when did a friend ever charge a friend interest? Instead, lend me this money as if you were lending it to an enemy — someone who, if he cannot repay the loan, you can happily require him to pay the penalty for breaking the contract."

Shylock replied, "Why, look how you storm! I want to be friends with you and have your respect. I want to forget the shames that you have caused me. I want to lend you the money you need and charge you not even a penny of interest. I want to do all these things, and you rail at me and will not listen to me. I am offering you a kindness."

"To lend us the money and not charge us interest is kindness indeed," Bassanio said.

"That is the kindness I am offering to you," Shylock said. "Go with me to a notary, and sign our contract there. I will not charge you interest. But as a merry joke, let us make the penalty for nonpayment of the money lent be exactly one pound of Antonio's fair flesh, to be cut off and taken from whatever part of Antonio's body it pleases me to take it."

"Indeed, I am satisfied and pleased with such a contract," Antonio said. "I will sign it, and I will say that you, Shylock, are kind."

More cautious and suspicious than Antonio, Bassanio said, "You shall not sign your name to such a contract for me. I would rather do without the money."

"Why, fear not, man," Antonio said. "I will not break the contract. Within the next two months — that's a whole month before this contract requires repayment — I expect my ships to return with nine times the amount of money I will borrow from Shylock."

Shylock said, "Oh, father Abraham, what kind of people are these Christians, whose own tough negotiations and business dealings teach them to suspect the thoughts of others!"

He said to Bassanio, "Please, tell me this. If Antonio should be unable to repay the loan, what should I gain by taking one pound of his flesh? A pound of flesh taken from a man is not as valuable or profitable as is the flesh of sheep, cattle, or goats. I say that in order to buy Antonio's favorable opinion of me I extend to him this friendship. If he will take it, well and good; if not, I commend him to God. And, if we are to be friends, I ask you to think that I do not have evil motives."

"Shylock," Antonio said, "I will sign the contract."

"Then go to the notary's and have him write up the contract. I will go and gather the ducats immediately, stop at my house to check on it because I left it in the unreliable hands of an unreliable servant, and very quickly I will go and meet you at the notary's."

"Hurry, gentle Jew," Antonio said.

Shylock departed, and Antonio said to Bassanio, "This Jew will convert and become a Christian; he grows kind and gentle — he even grows gentile."

"The terms of the contract seem to be fair, but I do not trust Shylock," Bassanio said. "I do not like the pairing of fair terms and a villainous mind."

"Come on," Antonio said. "In this contract there can be no dismay; my ships come home a month before the day I must repay the money."

CHAPTER 2

The Prince of Morocco entered a room of Portia's house in Belmont. The Prince was dark skinned and wore white clothing, as did the servants with him. Nerissa and a few servants were with Portia.

"Do not dislike me because of my dark complexion," the Prince of Morocco said. "My dark skin is the dark uniform of those who live beneath the shining Sun. I am a neighbor of and closely related to the Sun-god. Bring to me the fairest and lightest-skinned man born in the north, where the fire of the Sun scarcely thaws the icicles, and let both of us cut ourselves in a competition for your love. We two competitors will prove who has the redder blood: him or me. Red blood is a sign of courage. I tell you, lady, my red blood has made valiant men tremble in fear, and by my love for you I swear that the most admired virgins of my climate have loved my red blood. I would not change my complexion except to win your love, my gentle Queen."

"In deciding whom I shall love, I am not solely led by the over-particular criticism of a maiden's eyes," Portia said. "Besides, the lottery of my destiny prevents me from voluntarily choosing whom I shall marry; I shall marry whoever wins the lottery. But if my father had not restricted me and hedged me by his intelligence and his will, making me to yield myself and marry whoever chooses correctly among the three caskets that I have told you about, you, yourself, renowned Prince, would have as fair a chance of winning my voluntary love as any of the wooers whom I have seen so far."

"For that I thank you," the Prince of Morocco said. "Therefore, I ask you to lead me to the caskets so that I can try my luck. By this scimitar that slew the Shah of Persia and a Persian Prince who had defeated the Turkish Sultan Solyman the Magnificent in three battles, I would outstare the sternest eyes that look, outbrave the most daring heart on the Earth, pluck the young sucking cubs from the mother bear, yes, and mock the lion when he roars for prey, to win you, lady. But that is not how you must be won! If Hercules and his servant Lichas were to play at dice to determine which of the two is the better man, the best throw of the dice may — through sheer luck — come from the hand of the lesser man. In such a case, Hercules' servant would defeat Hercules. I, also, with blind fortune leading me, may miss that which a less worthy man may attain, and then I would die with grieving."

"If you are to win me as your wife, you must take your chance at choosing the correct casket. You can do one of two actions: You can decide not to choose any casket and depart unmarried, or, if you decide to choose a casket, you must swear that if you choose the wrong casket that you will never marry any lady. Therefore, carefully choose which action you will do."

"I will choose a casket, and if I choose the wrong casket, then I will never marry. Come, let me now make my choice among the three caskets."

"Not yet," Portia replied. "First, we must go to the temple where you can swear that if you choose the wrong casket then you will never marry. After we eat dinner, then you can choose one of the three caskets. That will be your hazardous choice."

"May I have good fortune when I choose a casket!" the Prince of Morocco said. "My choice will make me be blessed or cursed among men."

— 2.2 —

On a street in Venice, Launcelot Gobbo was talking to himself in front of Shylock's house. He was a rustic fellow from the country who had become a servant to Shylock, and he was a funny fellow who liked to play jokes and tease people and make them laugh or cry. Like his father, he sometimes misused words — often on purpose.

He said to himself, "Certainly my conscience will serve me to run away from this Jew who is my master. My conscience will tell me that running away is the right and ethical thing to do although ordinarily running away from one's master is the wrong and unethical thing to do.

"Let me put it to the test by imagining a conversation with my conscience and the Devil.

"The fiend — the Devil — is at my elbow and tempts me by saying to me, 'Gobbo, Launcelot Gobbo, good Launcelot, good Gobbo, good Launcelot Gobbo' — the Devil is a lawyer and wants to be sure to name me in such a way that I cannot pretend later that the Devil was talking to someone else.

"Anyway, the Devil says to me, 'Use your legs, take the start, run away.'

"But my conscience says, 'No; take heed,' honest Launcelot; take heed, honest Gobbo, or, as aforesaid, 'honest Launcelot Gobbo' — my conscience is also lawyer-like. It wants to name me in so many different ways so that later I cannot claim that my conscience was not speaking to me.

"Anyway, my conscience says, 'Do not run away, scorn running with your heels.'

"Well, the most courageous fiend — the Devil — advises me to pack in my job and run away. '*Fia*!' says the fiend. The Devil knows Italian, although he mispronounces it — By '*fia*,' the Devil means '*via*' or 'away!' The fiend tells me, 'In Heaven's name' — ha! The Devil said the word 'Heaven'! The Devil tells me, 'In Heaven's name, have a brave mind and run away.'

"Well, my conscience, hanging about the neck of my heart, says very wisely to me, 'My honest friend Launcelot, because you are an honest man's son' — but my conscience is wrong. I am not an honest man's son; rather, I am an honest woman's son. Indeed, my father did smack something — he kissed noisily with his lips something that may have been that area between a woman's legs. Then something else grew — something a little below his waist level. And then he had a kind of taste — his tongue and the thing that grew both tasted the same wetness. In short, my father cheated on his wife, and cheaters are not honest and so I am not an honest man's son.

"That reminds me. The Italian word '*fia*' can mean 'happening' or 'maybe' or, in northern Italy, 'vagina.'

"Well, my conscience says, 'Launcelot, budge not. Do not run away from your master.'

"The fiend, however, says, 'Budge. Run away from your master.'

"'Budge not,' says my conscience.

"'Conscience,' I say, 'you give good advice.'

"'Fiend,' I say, 'you also give good advice.'

"To be ruled by my conscience, I should stay with the Jew my master, who, if I may say so, is a kind of Devil.

"In order to run away from the Jew, I would have to take the advice of the fiend, who, if you will excuse me, is the Devil himself.

"Certainly the Jew is the very Devil incarnation — is that the right word? Should I say 'incarnate'?

"To speak truly, my conscience is a kind of hard conscience because it tells me to stay with the Jew.

"The fiend gives me the more friendly counsel — the advice that I want to hear.

"I will run, fiend; my heels are at your command; I will run. My conscience did not help me after all. The Devil is much friendlier to me than my conscience."

Launcelot was talking merely to amuse himself. He had already let Shylock know that he wanted to work for Bassanio, and Shylock had told him that he would talk to Bassanio and give him a good recommendation.

Before Launcelot Gobbo could run away, his father, Old Gobbo, who was nearly completely blind and was carrying a basket, arrived on the scene.

Old Gobbo asked Launcelot, "Master young man, please tell me which is the way to the house of master Shylock the Jew?"

Launcelot thought, *Heavens, this is my true-begotten father! To be stone-blind is to be completely blind. My father's eyesight is not as bad as that, but he is more blind than sand-blind, which is to be a little blind. It is better to call him gravel-blind and best to call him very gravel-blind because he is almost stone-blind. My father does not recognize me because his eyesight is so bad. I will try confusions with him — that should be funnier than to try conclusions with him. To try conclusions with someone means to argue with someone.*

Old Gobbo repeated, "Master young gentleman, please tell me which is the way to master Jew's house."

Launcelot and his father were standing in front of Shylock's house, but Launcelot turned his father in all directions as he said, "Turn to your right hand at the next turning, but at the next turning, turn to your left. At the turning after that, do not turn at all, but instead move at an angle to the Jew's house."

When Launcelot had finished turning his father in all directions, his father was facing the door of Shylock's house.

"By God's saints, it will be difficult for me to find the Jew's house," Old Gobbo said. "Can you tell me whether a certain man named Launcelot, who works for him, dwells with him or not?"

"Are you speaking of young Master Launcelot?" Launcelot asked.

He thought, *This is an opportunity for me to raise the waters and bring tears to my father's eyes.*

"Launcelot is no master, sir. A master is a man of a higher status than Launcelot has ever achieved; he is only a poor man's son. His father, even if it is

I who say it, is an honest and exceedingly poor man and, God be thanked, well to live. He is so poor that he does well even to live, being unable to live well."

"Well, let his father be what his father will," Launcelot said. "Instead, let us talk about young Master Launcelot."

"Let us talk about Launcelot. We have no reason to bring 'master' into our conversation."

"Please, old man, ergo, old man, ergo, I ask you, are you talking about young Master Launcelot?"

He thought, *One of these days I need to find out what "ergo" means. I have heard many learned men use it — and use it and use it.*

Old Gobbo said, "I am talking about Launcelot, not Master Launcelot, if it pleases your mastership."

"Ergo, Master Launcelot is the subject of our conversation. Don't talk about Master Launcelot, father — you don't mind if I call you 'father,' do you? An old man such as yourself must be a father. As I was saying, don't talk about Master Launcelot because the young gentleman, according to Fates and Destinies and such odd sayings and prophecies, and according to the Sisters Three who are the Three Fates who control the destinies of men, and according to such branches of learning, is indeed deceased, or, as you would say in plain terms, he has gone to Heaven."

"God forbid!" Old Gobbo said. "The boy was the very staff of my old age, my very prop, the person who supported me."

Launcelot, who was fat, not thin, said, "Do I look like a long, thin cudgel or a long, thin hovel-post or a long, thin staff or a long, thin prop? Do you know me, father? And by 'father,' I mean 'father' as in 'biological father.'"

"I do not know you, young gentleman, but, please tell me for real about my boy, God rest his soul. Is he alive or dead?"

"Seriously, don't you know me, father?"

"Alas, sir, I am sand-blind; I do not know you."

"Indeed, even if you had good eyes, you might fail to recognize me: It is a wise father who knows his own child. Well, old man, I will tell you news about your son."

Launcelot knelt and added, "Give me your blessing. Truth will come to light; murder cannot be hid long; a man's son may be unrecognized for a while, but sooner or later the truth will come out. So, father, give me your blessing. You can safely bless me. I am no Jacob."

Genesis 27 tells how Jacob deceived Isaac, the father of Esau and him, into giving him a blessing intended for Esau.

"Please, sir, stand up," Old Gobbo said. "I am sure you are not Launcelot, my boy."

"Please, father," Launcelot said, "let's have no more fooling about it — quickly give me your blessing: I am Launcelot, your boy who was, your son who is, your child who shall be."

"I cannot believe you are my son."

"I don't know what I shall think about that, but I am Launcelot, Shylock the Jew's servant, and I am sure Margery, your wife, is my mother."

"My wife's name is Margery, indeed," Old Gobbo said. "I'll be sworn, if you really are Launcelot, you are my own flesh and blood. The Lord be praised if you are!"

Old Gobbo reached out his hand and felt the long hair on the back of Launcelot's head and said, "What a beard you have got! You have more hair on your chin than Dobbin my carthorse has on his tail."

"It should seem, then, that Dobbin's tail grows backward," Launcelot said. "It grows shorter, not longer. I am sure Dobbin had more hair on his tail than I have on my face when I last saw him."

"Lord, how you have changed! But you are my son. How do you and your master get along? I have brought him a present. Do you and your master get along well?"

"We get along well — yes, well. But, so far as I am concerned, as I have set up my rest to run away — that is, I have made up my mind to run away — so I will not rest until I have run some distance and put some ground between my master and me. My master is a stereotypical Jew. You want to give him a present! Instead, give him a halter with which he can hang himself. I am famished in his service; he starves me," Launcelot said, bouncing on his toes and jiggling his fat belly.

He added, "Most people use their fingers to help them count. I use my ribs to count my fingers! Father, I am glad you have come. Give your present to a certain Master Bassanio, who, indeed, gives very nice new uniforms to his servants. If I do not become one of his servants, I will run away as far as God has any ground."

He looked around and said, "Here is some good luck! Here comes Master Bassanio walking toward us. Speak to him, father, for I am a Jew if I serve the Jew any longer."

Bassanio, his servant Leonardo, and some other servants walked close to Launcelot Gobbo and Old Gobbo.

Bassanio said to a servant, "You may do so, but let it be done so hastily that supper will be ready no later than five o'clock. See to it that these letters are delivered, get the uniforms made, and tell Gratiano to come at once to my lodging."

Launcelot said, "Talk to him, father."

"God bless your worship!" Old Gobbo said.

"God bless you!" Bassanio replied. "How may I help you?"

"This is my son, sir, a poor boy — "

Launcelot interrupted, "I am not a poor boy, sir. Instead, I am the rich Jew's man, or servant. I would, sir, as my father will tell you — "

Old Gobbo said, "He has a great infection, sir, as one would say, to serve — "

Bassanio thought, *A great infection? He means "ambition."*

Launcelot interrupted, "Indeed, the short and the long of it is, I serve the Jew, and I have a desire, as my father will tell you — "

Old Gobbo said, "His master and he, if you don't mind my saying so, are scarcely cater-cousins — they are hardly close friends who eat together — "

Launcelot interrupted, "To be brief, the very truth is that the Jew, having done me wrong, does cause me, as my father, being, I hope, an old man, shall frutify unto you — "

Bassanio thought, *Frutify? He means "notify," I think. To fructify is to bear fruit.*

Old Gobbo said, "I have here a dish of doves prepared for eating that I would bestow upon your worship, and my suit or request is — "

Launcelot interrupted, "To be very brief, the suit is impertinent to myself, as your worship shall know by this honest old man; and, I must say it, this old man, this poor man, is my father."

Bassanio thought, *Impertinent? I can guess that he means "pertinent."*

Bassanio said, "Just one of you do all the speaking for both of you. What do you want?"

Launcelot said, "I want to work for you, sir."

Old Gobbo said, "That is the very defect of the matter, sir."

Bassanio thought, *Defect? I can guess that he means "effect" or "purport."*

"I know who you are now," Bassanio said. "Yes, you can work for me. Shylock, your master, spoke with me today, and he gave you a good recommendation. But I wonder whether you are doing the right thing: Is it wise to stop working for a rich Jew and start working for so impoverished a gentleman as me?"

Launcelot replied, "Let us remember this old proverb: He who has the grace of God has enough. We can split the proverb in two and apply it to the Jew and you. As a Christian, you have the grace of God; as a rich Jew, Shylock has enough when it comes to money."

"You speak well," Bassanio said to Launcelot. "You have a mastery of words and can use — or willfully misuse — them well."

He said to Old Gobbo, "Go, father, with your son."

He said to Launcelot, "Say goodbye to your old master and then go to my lodging."

He said to one of his other servants, "Give Launcelot a uniform different from that of the other servants. Give him the uniform of a jester. He shall be my fool."

Launcelot smiled. This was a promotion. He would no longer be an ordinary servant but would instead use his brain and wit to entertain Bassanio and make him laugh.

Launcelot said to his father, "Father, we will go inside the Jew's house."

He then started in on his new job: "I am a failure. I cannot get a job as an ordinary servant because I cannot speak correctly. Well, let me read my palm. I hold it flat like a table, and I do not think that any other man in Italy has a better table to place a Bible on — or to place on a Bible — and swear to tell the truth, the whole truth, and nothing but the truth. If any man does have a better table, well, I shall have good luck anyway. Ah, yes, the table line in palmistry is the line of fortune. Let me look at the lines on my palm. Ah, here is an unremarkable lifeline, but I see leading to it long, deep lines from the thumb's ball, aka the Mount of Venus. Those lines indicate how many wives I will have. Nothing remarkable, I see. Here is a small trifling number of wives — alas, fifteen wives is nothing! Eleven widows and nine maidens is a simple coming-in for one man. If I collect dowries, I will have money coming-in, and I will also have wives for cumming-in. I see that I will escape being drowned twice and so escape the peril of water, but I will be in peril of losing my life while I am on the edge of a featherbed. I see sexcapades and marital escapades in my life, but these are unremarkable sex adventures. Well, if Fortune is a woman, she's a good wench for having given me this palm. Father, let us go. I will take my leave of the Jew in the twinkling of an eye."

Launcelot Gobbo and his father went into Shylock's house.

Bassanio returned to business, saying, "Good Leonardo, look at this list. Buy these things and stow them neatly on board ship, but return quickly, for I am hosting a feast tonight for my best friends. Go now, and hurry."

"I will do my best," Leonardo said and then departed.

Gratiano now came walking toward Leonardo and asked, "Where is your master, Bassanio?"

"There he is, sir," Leonardo said, pointing.

Gratiano called, "Signior Bassanio!"

Bassanio replied, "Hello, Gratiano."

Gratiano walked over to Bassanio and said, "I have a favor to ask of you."

"Whatever it is, I will grant it."

"You must not say no to me; I must go with you to Belmont."

"Why, then you must," Bassanio said. "But listen to me, Gratiano, you are too wild and too rude and too bold of voice. These are qualities that become you happily enough, and in such eyes as mine and those of your other friends, these qualities do not appear to be faults. But in places where you are not known, why, there they seem to be too free and open and unrestrained and liberal. Please, be careful to use some cold drops of modesty to lessen your thoughtless and boisterous and skipping spirit, lest through your wild behavior people will think badly of me in the place I go to, thus making me lose all my hopes of marrying a deceased rich man's daughter."

"Signior Bassanio, listen to me," Gratiano said. "If I do not put on a sober covering, both of clothing and behavior, talk with respect and swear only now and then, carry prayer-books in my pockets, appear to be demure and modest, and while prayers are being said at the dinner table, if I do not take off my hat and use it to cover my eyes, and if I do not sigh and say, 'Amen,' and if I do not always observe good etiquette, like a person who customarily assumes a serious expression in order to please his grandmother, then never trust me more."

"Well, we shall see how you act when the time for good behavior comes."

"No problem, but tonight does not count. Do not judge me by how I act tonight in your presence."

"OK," Bassanio said. "It would be a pity if you were sober and serious tonight. Instead, I urge you to put on your boldest suit of mirth, for we have friends who wish to be merry with us. But goodbye for now — I have some business to take care of."

"And I must go to Lorenzo and the others," Gratiano said, "but we will visit you at suppertime."

— 2.3 —

Launcelot Gobbo, who was now working as the fool of Bassanio, was talking in front of Shylock's house with Jessica, who was the daughter of Shylock.

Jessica said, "I am sorry that you are no longer going to work for my father and will instead work for a new master: Bassanio. Our house is Hell, and you, who are a merry Devil, did rob it of some of its tedium and boredom. But farewell, and here is a ducat for you. One more thing. Launcelot, soon at supper you shall see Lorenzo, who is your new master's guest. Give him this letter; do it secretly, and so farewell. I do not want my father to see me talking with you. He might suspect something."

"Adieu!" Launcelot said. "Tears exhibit my tongue. My tongue need not express my sorrow because my tears are already doing that. You are a very beautiful pagan and a very sweet Jew! If a Christian does not play the knave and steal you away from your father to be his wife, I am much deceived. But, adieu. These foolish drops on my cheeks do somewhat drown my manly spirit. Adieu."

"Farewell, good Launcelot."

Carrying the letter that Jessica had given to him, Launcelot departed to go to Bassanio, his new employer.

Jessica said, "I am committing a heinous sin by being ashamed of Shylock, my father! I am ashamed to be my father's child! But although I am his daughter and therefore I share his blood, I do not share his manners. I inherited his blood, but not his behavior. Oh, Lorenzo, if you keep the promise you made

26

to me, I shall end this strife by becoming a Christian and your loving wife. If I become your wife, two will become one, and I will share your blood and not my father's."

She went inside her father's house.

— 2.4 —

Gratiano, Lorenzo, Salarino, and Solanio now walked near Shylock's house and then stopped to talk.

Lorenzo was making plans for them that night to attend Bassanio's masquerade ball: "At suppertime, we will sneak away, go to my lodging, disguise ourselves with masks, and return and make a grand entrance with torchbearers and musicians, all within one hour."

Gratiano objected, "We have not made good preparation."

Salarino brought up an example: "We have not yet hired torchbearers to accompany us as we go to the masquerade ball."

Solanio said, "It would be bad to do as you suggest unless we can do it properly and with style; if we cannot, then it is better not to do it."

Lorenzo pointed out, "It is now only four o'clock: we have two hours to get everything ready."

Launcelot now arrived, carrying the letter that Jessica had given to him to give to Lorenzo.

Lorenzo asked, "Launcelot, what news do you have for us?"

"If it will please you to break the seal on this letter, you may read for yourself what's the news."

Launcelot gave Lorenzo the letter, and Lorenzo looked at it and said, "I know the handwriting. Truly, the hand that wrote it is a pretty hand and whiter than the paper it wrote on."

"It must be a love letter," Gratiano said.

Launcelot said, "Please excuse me, sir. I must leave."

"Where are you going?" Lorenzo asked.

"I am ordered to invite my old master the Jew to eat tonight with my new master the Christian."

"Wait a moment," Lorenzo said. "Here is a tip for you. Tell gentle Jessica that I will not fail to see her. Tell my message to her privately."

Launcelot departed.

Lorenzo said, "Gentlemen, will you prepare yourselves to wear masks for this masquerade ball tonight? I will have a torchbearer."

He had read the letter and knew that Jessica, disguised as a young male, would be their torchbearer.

Salarino said, "Yes, indeed, I will start my preparations now."

Solanio said, "And so will I."

Lorenzo said, "Meet Gratiano and me at Gratiano's lodging one hour from now."

Salarino said. "Good. We will do so."

Salarino and Solanio departed.

Gratiano asked, "Wasn't that letter from beautiful Jessica?"

"I will tell you everything," Lorenzo said. "She has given me instructions for how I can take her from her father's house. In the letter she has also told me how much gold and how many jewels she has. She also wrote that she intends to disguise herself by wearing the clothing of a page: a young male servant.

"If ever the Jew her father goes to Heaven, it will be for his gentle daughter's sake. Misfortune would never dare to cross her path unless it should do so because she is the daughter of a Jew: one who does not have Christian faith."

"Come, go with me; read Jessica's letter as we walk. Fair Jessica shall be my torchbearer tonight."

They departed.

— 2.5 —

Launcelot and Shylock were talking in front of Shylock's house.

"Well, you shall see — your own eyes will show you — the difference between old Shylock and Bassanio," Shylock said to Launcelot.

Shylock called for his daughter, who was inside his house: "Jessica!"

He said to Launcelot, "With Bassanio, you shall not be able to gourmandize and eat like a glutton the way that you have been doing here."

He shouted, "Jessica!"

He said to Launcelot, "With Bassanio, you shall not be able to sleep and snore and wear out your clothing."

He shouted, "Jessica!"

Launcelot now shouted, "Jessica!"

Shylock asked, "Who asked you to call for her? I did not ask you to call for her."

"Your worship was accustomed to tell me that I could do nothing without first being ordered to do it."

Jessica came out of the house and asked her father, "Were you calling for me? What can I do for you?"

"I have been invited to supper, Jessica," Shylock said. "Here are my keys. But why should I eat supper with Bassanio and Antonio? They have not invited me out of friendship. This is a form of flattering me. But yet I'll go in hate, and not in friendship, to feed upon the food of Bassanio, the prodigal Christian. Jessica, my girl, look after my house. I am very loath to leave here and go to the supper. There is some ill brewing that will disturb my rest. I know that because I dreamed of moneybags last night — an ill omen!"

"Please, let us leave," Launcelot said. "Bassanio, my young master, expects your reproach."

"You probably meant to say that Bassanio expects my approach," Shylock said, "But your words, even when wrongly chosen, are often apt. He expects my reproach, and I expect his. Each of us expects the displeasure of the other's company."

Launcelot said, "I believe that they have conspired together. I will not say that you shall see a masquerade, but if you do, then it was not for nothing that I have experienced bad omens."

He then began to parody such ill omens as dreaming of moneybags: "My nose bled on the most recent Black Monday at six o'clock in the morning, and just four years ago I got a nosebleed on Ash Wednesday in the afternoon. Black Monday is especially ominous. It is the day after Easter, and the Black Monday of 1360 was so cold that many men died as they rode on horseback. Dreams are especially prescient on feast days, and Black Monday is the day after a feast day and so it is maybe possibly sort of prescient."

"What, is there going to be a masquerade ball?" Shylock said. "I hate such frivolity. Listen to me, Jessica. Lock up the doors of the house, and when you hear the drum and the vile squealing of the fife by musicians who must twist their necks awry to play the instrument, do not climb up to the upper story's windows or thrust your head out of the window to gaze on Christian fools with masked faces. Instead, stop my house's ears — I mean close the shutters — to keep out the noises and noisome music. Do not allow the sound of shallow frivolity to enter my sober house. By Jacob's staff — the staff that was his main possession when he crossed the river Jordan and then made himself a wealthy man — I swear that I do not wish to leave my house and feast away from home tonight. However, I will go. Launcelot, you go now and tell your master that I will come to his feast."

"I will, sir," Launcelot said.

To Jessica, Launcelot said quietly, "Mistress, look out the window, despite what your father said. There will come a Christian who will be worth a look from you, a Jew."

Launcelot departed.

Shylock asked his daughter, "What did that fool, that offspring of Hagar, say to you? Abraham rejected Hagar and her offspring — her son, Ishmael — and sent them away, I am as contemptuous of Launcelot right now as Abraham was of Hagar and her son."

Jessica said, "He said, 'Farewell, mistress,' and nothing more."

Shylock said, "Launcelot is a patch — a fool. He is kind enough, but he is a huge eater, he is as slow as a snail when it comes to learning how to do his job, and he sleeps by day more than a nocturnal wildcat that stays awake all night. He is like a drone: a male bee that does no work. Well, I do not allow drones to hive — to live — with me, and therefore I part with him, and I part with him to one who will let him help to waste the money he has borrowed from me.

"Well, Jessica, go inside. Perhaps I will return very quickly. Do as I told you. Lock the doors after you are inside. Remember this proverb that thrifty minds ought always to remember: Fast bind, fast find. Keep your things locked up, and thieves will steal them not. Lock everything up tight, and everything will be all right. Keep safe what you've got, and you shall lack for naught."

Shylock departed.

Jessica said quietly, "Farewell. Unless my fortune is crossed with bad luck, I will lose a father and you will lose a daughter."

She went inside the house.

— 2.6 —

Gratiano and Salarino, both of them wearing masks, walked up to Shylock's house.

Gratiano said, "This is the slanting and overhanging roof under which Lorenzo wanted us to stand and wait for him."

Salarino said, "He ought to be here by now. He is late."

"It is a marvel that he is late. Lovers are usually early when they are meeting the one they love."

"The doves that draw the chariot of Venus, goddess of love, fly ten times faster when they carry new lovers than when they carry long-married faithful couples!"

"That has always been the case," Gratiano said. "Who stands up after feasting with the same appetite that he had when he sat down to feast? Where is the horse that runs back with the same energy that it had when it started its race? Everything is better when it is anticipated than when it is enjoyed. A ship hung with sails and banners sets forth from its home bay like a young prodigal son who sets out from home. Both are hugged and embraced by wantons — the ship's sails are hugged by wanton winds, and the young men are hugged by wanton women. But the ship returns like the prodigal son — its wooden ribs are now weather-beaten timbers and its proud sails are now ragged. The sails and the prodigal son are lean and torn, and they have been beggared by wantons."

"Here comes Lorenzo," Salarino said. "We will talk more about this later."

Lorenzo said, "Sweet friends, thank you for your patience as you waited for me. I know that I am late. Not I, but some business that came up, have made you wait. When you shall want to play the thieves to acquire wives, I'll wait as long for you then as you have waited for me now. Let us go to this door. This is where my soon-to-be father-in-law the Jew lives."

He said loudly, "Who is inside this house?"

Jessica, dressed in male clothing, appeared on a second-floor balcony.

She said, "Who are you? Tell me so that I can know for certain, although I would swear that I recognize your voice."

"I am Lorenzo, and I am the man you love."

"You are Lorenzo for certain, and you are indeed the man I love. Who do I love as much as I love you? No one. And who knows better than you, Lorenzo, whether I am yours?"

"Heaven and your own thoughts are witnesses that you are mine," Lorenzo replied.

"Here, catch this box," Jessica said. "It is worth the trouble of catching it. I am glad it is night so that you cannot see me because I am very ashamed of the clothing I am wearing — I have exchanged my woman's clothing for a man's clothing. But love is blind and lovers cannot see the pretty follies that they themselves commit; if they could, Cupid himself would blush to see me thus transformed to a boy."

"Come down because you must be my torchbearer," Lorenzo said.

"What, must I hold a candle to illuminate my shame? My shame in itself, truly, is too apparent and too immodest. Lorenzo, my love, you know that torches shed a light on things, and I really ought to be hidden by darkness."

"You are sweet and lovely even when you are disguised and clothed like a boy, but come at once because the secretive night is acting like a runaway as it quickly steals away. People are waiting for us at the feast of Bassanio."

"I will lock the doors and gild myself with gold by taking some more gold ducats and be with you quickly," Jessica said.

Gratiano said, "I give my word that she is a gentle and well-born gentile and not a Jew. Her behavior shows that."

"I am lying if I do not say I love her heartily," Lorenzo said. "She is wise, if I can judge her fairly, and she is beautiful, if my eyes tell me the truth, and she is faithful to me, as she has proven herself to be by her actions, and therefore, she, who is wise, beautiful, and faithful, shall have a place in my heart and in my soul. Our masked friends are at the masquerade ball waiting for us."

Jessica came out of her father's house.

Lorenzo said, "Good, you are here. Gentlemen, let us leave."

Lorenzo, Jessica, and Salarino departed. Gratiano started to leave with them, but he saw Antonio coming and instead walked to meet him.

"Who's there?" Antonio said.

"Antonio, it is I!"

"Gratiano! Where are all the others? It is nine o'clock: Our friends are all waiting for you. There will be no masque for you tonight. The wind has changed and is favorable for sailing. Bassanio will go on board very quickly. I have sent twenty men out to look for you."

"I am glad that the wind has changed," Gratiano said. "I desire no more delight than to set sail and be gone tonight."

— 2.7 —

In a room in her home, Portia was standing with the Prince of Morocco and several servants, both hers and his.

Portia said to one of her servants, "Draw the curtains and show this noble Prince the three caskets."

She then said to the Prince of Morocco, "Now make your choice."

He said, "The first casket, which is made of gold, has this inscription: '*Whoever chooses me shall gain what many men desire.*'

"The second casket, which is made of silver, is inscribed with this promise: '*Whoever chooses me shall get as much as he deserves.*'

"The third casket, which is made of dull lead, is inscribed with this warning that is as unpolished and plain as the lead of the casket: '*Whoever chooses me must give and hazard all he has.*'

"How shall I know if I have chosen the right casket?"

Portia replied, "One of the caskets contains my picture, Prince. If you choose that casket, then I am yours and we shall be married."

"May some god help me to choose the right casket!" the Prince of Morocco said. "Let me see; I will read the inscriptions again.

"What does this lead casket say? '*Whoever chooses me must give and hazard all he has.*' Give all he has? For what? For lead? Hazard all he has? For lead? The inscription of this casket is threatening. Men who hazard all they have do so in hope of good returns. A golden mind does not lower itself for displays of worthless dross; therefore, I will neither give nor hazard anything for lead.

"What says the silver casket with her virgin hue? Silver is the color of the Moon, whose goddess is the virgin Diana. '*Whoever chooses me shall get as much as he deserves.*' As much as he deserves! Pause there, Prince of Morocco, and weigh your value with an impartial hand. If you should be judged by your self-esteem, you certainly are deserving enough, and yet 'enough' may not extend so far as to this lady, Portia. And yet to be unsure of what I deserve is a weak belittling of myself. As much as I deserve! Why, I deserve the lady! I do deserve her because of my birth, because of my fortunes, because of my graces, and because of my qualities of breeding. But more than any of these, I do deserve her because of my love. What if I looked no further, but simply chose the silver casket?

"Let's see once more this saying that is engraved on the gold casket: '*Whoever chooses me shall gain what many men desire.*' Why, many men desire the lady; all the world desires her; from the four corners of the Earth, they come to kiss this shrine, this mortal-breathing saint: The wild Hyrcanian deserts and the vast wildernesses of wide Arabia are like thoroughfares now for Princes to come to view fair Portia. The watery kingdom that is the ocean, whose ambitious head — the tall waves — spits in the face of Heaven, is no bar to stop the foreign spirited men of courage, for they come as if they were traveling over a mere brook to see fair Portia.

"One of these three caskets contains her Heavenly picture.

"Is it likely that the lead casket contains her picture? It would be a damnable offense to think so base a thought: it would be too gross to think that. Should her picture be wrapped in a lead casket as if for burial? Is she to be wrapped in lead for burial in a dark grave?

"Or shall I think she would be wrapped in silver for burial? But silver is worth only one-tenth as much as gold. It is sinful to think that her picture would be in a silver casket. Portia is a rich gem, and such a rich gem would be set only in gold. They have in England a coin that bears the figure of an angel stamped in gold, but that is only an engraving. But here the picture of an angel lies in a golden bed — the gold casket.

"Give me the key to the gold casket. That is the casket I choose. Let us see whether I will be successful."

"Here is the key," Portia said. "If my picture is inside the gold casket, then I am yours."

The Prince of Morocco unlocked the gold casket and opened it.

"Oh, Hell!" he said. "What have we here? A carrion Death's head, a skull, within whose empty eye socket there is a written scroll! I'll read the writing out loud:

"All that glitters is not gold;
"Often have you heard that told:
"Many a man his life has sold
"Only my outside to behold.
"Gilded tombs do worms enfold.
"Had you been as wise as bold,
"Young in limbs, in judgment old,
"Your answer had not been inscrolled.
"Instead, you would have seen a picture.
"Farewell; your hopes are dead and cold.

"My hopes are dead and cold indeed, and my labor is lost. Farewell, heat, and welcome, frost! Portia, adieu. I have too grieved a heart to take a long and tedious leave; losers leave quickly."

The Prince of Morocco departed with his servants.

Portia said, "Good riddance. Draw the curtains closed. I hope that everyone with his complexion and character will choose a casket with the same success that he did. He has too great an opinion of himself and suffers from excessive self-esteem."

— 2.8 —

On a street in Venice, Salarino and Solanio were talking.

Salarino said, "Why, man, I saw Bassanio under sail. Gratiano set sail with him, but I am sure that Lorenzo did not set sail with them."

Solanio said, "The villain Jew with his outcries got the Duke out of bed. They went together to search Bassanio's ship for Jessica and the money and jewels she took with her."

"They came too late to search the ship," Salarino said. "The ship had already set sail. But there the Duke was told that Lorenzo and his amorous Jessica were seen together in a gondola. In addition, Antonio swore to the Duke that Lorenzo and Jessica were not on board that ship."

"I never heard passionate cries so confused, so strange, so outrageous, and so variable as those the dog Jew did shout in the streets: 'My daughter! Oh, my ducats! Oh, my daughter! Fled with a Christian! Oh, my Christian ducats! Justice! The law! My ducats, and my daughter! A sealed bag, two sealed bags of ducats, of double ducats worth twice as much as ordinary ducats, stolen from me by my daughter! And jewels, two stones, two rich and precious stones, stolen by my daughter! Justice! Find the girl. She has the stones with her, and she has the ducats.'"

"Why, all the boys in Venice followed him," Salarino said. "They were shouting, 'His stones, his daughter, and his ducats.' They were laughing, knowing as they did that the word 'stones' can mean testicles as well as jewels."

Solanio said, "Antonio must be very careful and be very sure to pay back his loan to Shylock on the day it is due, or Shylock will use the breach of contract to get revenge on Antonio for this. The Jew's daughter ran away with Antonio's friend."

"That is true," Salarino said. "I just remembered something. I talked with a Frenchman yesterday, who told me that in the narrow sea that parts the French and the English — the English Channel — there miscarried a richly loaded vessel of our country. It wrecked and all its cargo was lost. I thought about Antonio when the Frenchman told me this, and I silently hoped that the wrecked ship was not one of his."

"It is best for you to tell Antonio what you heard, but do not tell him suddenly because the bad news may make him grieve."

"No kinder gentleman than Antonio treads the Earth," Salarino said. "I saw Bassanio and Antonio part. Bassanio told him he would hurry and return home again, but Antonio replied, 'Do not hurry. Do not rush things for my sake, Bassanio. Instead, take your time and do things the right way at the right time. And as for the contract that I made with the Jew to borrow money, do not let it bother you. Instead, think about wooing Portia and being in love. Be merry, and chiefly think about courtship and such fair demonstrations of love as shall conveniently become you there.' Antonio's eyes were big with tears. Turning his face away, he put his arm around Bassanio, and with touching affection he shook Bassanio's hand; and so they parted."

"I think that Bassanio is the reason Antonio stays alive," Solanio said. "And now, let us go and find Antonio so that we can cheer him up. He is indulging too much in sadness."

"Good idea," Salarino said. "Let's do that."

— 2.9 —

Nerissa and a servant entered the room with the three caskets.

She said, "Quick, quick, please draw the curtain immediately. The Prince of Arragon has taken his oath, and he is coming here to make his choice of caskets."

Portia, the Prince of Arragon, and some servants, both hers and his, entered the room.

"Look, here are the three caskets, noble Prince," Portia said. "If you chose the casket that contains my picture, you and I shall be immediately married, but if you fail to choose the right casket, then you must leave immediately with no arguing."

"I have sworn an oath to do three things if I fail to choose the right casket," the Prince of Arragon said. "I must never tell anyone which casket I chose, I must never get married, and I must leave you immediately."

"Those are the three things that everyone must swear if they come here and attempt to win my worthless self."

"And those are the three things that I have sworn. May Fortune lead me now to what my heart hopes for!

"The three caskets are made of gold, silver, and base lead.

"The lead casket says, '*Whoever chooses me must give and hazard all he has.*' Well, lead casket, you must be more beautiful before I give and hazard all I have for you.

"What does the gold casket say? Let me see. '*Whoever chooses me shall gain what many men desire.*' What many men desire! That phrase 'many men' may refer to the multitude of fools, who choose according to a showy exterior and do not seek to learn more than their foolish eyes show them. But eyes see only the exterior and not the interior. They do not see everything and so cannot always help a person make the best decision. People who choose on the basis of a flashy exterior are like those birds called swifts that build their nests on the sides of buildings and so expose their nestlings to bad weather. I will not choose what many men desire because I will not go along with common spirits and will not classify myself as one of the barbarous multitudes.

"Why, then let me look at you, you silver treasure house. Tell me once more what is engraved on you. '*Whoever chooses me shall get as much as he deserves.*' That is well said because who shall go about to try to cheat fortune and be honorable without the stamp of merit? Let no one presume to wear an undeserved dignity. I wish that estates of the realm such as nobility, ranks such as Earls and Barons, and offices that are official appointments such as the Chancellorship were not obtained corruptly. I wish that the merit of the man is what would get the man magnificent and glorious honor. If that were so, many men who now wear hats in the presence of other, better men would remove their hats and stand bareheaded to show respect to the other, better men! Many men who now give orders would instead be obeying orders! Many men who are now nobles would instead be peasants! And many men who are now the lowest of the low and ruined by bad times would be among the highest of the high!

"Well, which casket shall I choose? '*Whoever chooses me shall get as much as he deserves.*' I will assume that I am deserving of this lady. Give me the key to the silver casket, and I will immediately unlock it and find my fortune."

The Prince of Arragon opened the silver casket and stood silently.

Portia said, "You are pausing for a long time. I assume that you do not like what you see."

"What's this?" the Prince of Arragon said. "Here is the portrait of a goggle-eyed idiot presenting to me a scroll! I will read it. This portrait is much unlike Portia. It is much unlike what I hoped to find here and much unlike what I deserved to find here! '*Whoever chooses me shall have as much as he deserves.*' Do I deserve to have no more than a fool's head? Is that my prize? Do I deserve to have no better?"

"The guilty person on trial and the fair judge are two separate people. They ought not to do each other's jobs," Portia said.

The Prince of Arragon said, "What is here on the scroll? I will read it out loud:

"*The fire has seven times tested*
"*And purified this silver casket.*
"*Seven times tested that judgment is,*
"*That did never choose amiss.*
"*Some there be that shadows kiss.*
"*Such have but a shadow's bliss.*
"*There be fools alive, certainly,*
"*Whose foolishness is hidden by silver,*
"*Whether by silver hair or a wealth of silver coins.*
"*This casket's interior was hidden by silver.*
"*Take what wife you will to bed,*
"*Fools do not keep their oaths,*
"*I will ever be your fool's head:*
"*So be gone: you have been well dealt with.*

"I shall appear to be even more of a fool if I longer linger here. With one fool's head I came to woo, but I go away with two. Sweet, adieu. I'll keep my oath, and I will patiently bear my sorrow."

The Prince of Arragon and his attendants departed.

Portia said, "The Prince of Arragon was a fool, and thus has the candle singed the moth. Oh, these deliberating fools! When they choose, they choose wrongly. The fools' reasoning gives them the wisdom to choose the wrong casket."

Nerissa said, "This ancient saying is no heresy: Hanging and wiving go by destiny. Whether or not we are hung is destined, and whom we marry or not marry is also destined."

Portia said, "Draw the curtain shut, Nerissa."

A servant entered and asked, "Where is my lady?"

Portia replied, "Here I am," then she joked, referring to the servant, "What does my lord want?"

"Madam, there has alighted at your gate a young Venetian man, one who comes before to let us know that his lord is coming. From his lord he has brought greetings: compliments, polite speeches, and gifts of rich value. I have never seen so promising and handsome an ambassador of love. This young Venetian man is like a sweet day in April. The April day foretells a summer that is rich in flowers, and this young Venetian man foretells a lord who promises to be a worthy husband."

"Say no more, please," Portia said to the servant. "I am half afraid that you will say soon that he is a relative of yours because you are using such elegant language to praise him."

She added, "Come, Nerissa; I long to see quick Cupid's messenger who comes so courteously."

"I hope that he is the messenger of Bassanio," Nerissa said. "Cupid, god of love, so let it be so, if you will it so."

CHAPTER 3

— 3.1 —

On a street in Venice, Solanio and Salarino were talking.

Solanio said, "What is the news that you have heard at the merchants' exchange?"

"The rumor persists — with no one contradicting it — that one of Antonio's merchant ships has wrecked on the narrow seas," Salarino said. "People say that it wrecked on the Goodwin Sands in the English Channel. The Goodwin Sands is a very dangerous and fatal sandbank where the carcasses of many gallant ships lie buried. If my old friend and gossip Dame Rumor is an honest woman of her word, Antonio has suffered a grievous loss."

"I would say that Dame Rumor were as lying a gossip in saying that as any old woman who ever munched ginger cookies or made her neighbors believe she wept for the death of a third husband," Solanio said. "But it is true, without any slips of prolixity or crossing the plain highway of talk or taking way too many words to say a simple thing, that the good Antonio, the honest Antonio — oh, I wish that I had a title that was good enough to put in front of his name! — "

"Please," Salarino said. "Finish your sentence. Take your words from a gallop to a full stop."

"Ha! Funny!" Solanio said. "But the end of my sentence is that Antonio has lost one of his merchant ships."

"I hope that one ship is all that he will lose."

"Let me say 'Amen!' quickly," Solanio said, "lest the Devil frustrate my prayer, for here the Devil comes in the likeness of a Jew."

Shylock walked up to them, and Solanio said, "How are you, Shylock! What news do you hear among the merchants?"

"You know — no one knows as well as you — of my daughter's flight," Shylock replied.

"That's the truth," Salarino said. "I, for my part, knew the tailor who made the wings your daughter used to fly away with."

"And Shylock, for his own part, knew that the bird was fledged and ready to fly, and when a bird is fledged it is eager to leave home," Solanio said.

"My daughter is damned for what she did," Shylock said.

"That's the truth," Salarino said, "if the Devil is judging her."

"My own flesh and blood rebelled against me!" Shylock said.

"You don't say, old, old man!" Solanio said. "Your own flesh and blood rebelled against you! At your advanced age, how was your penis able to rise up against you!"

"I say," Shylock said, "that my daughter is my flesh and blood."

"There is more difference between your flesh and hers than there is between jet black and ivory white," Salarino said. "There is more difference between your bloods than there is between bad red wine and good Rhenish white wine. But tell us, have you heard whether Antonio has had any losses at sea or not?"

"There I have made another bad bargain," Shylock said. "Antonio is a bankrupt, a prodigal, a man who scarcely dares to show his head at the merchants' exchange. He is a beggar, he who used to come so smugly and self-satisfied to the marketplace. Let him remember that he has a contract with me and that he must not renege on it! Antonio has been accustomed to call me a usurer. Let him remember that he has a contract with me and that he must not renege on it! He was accustomed to lend money at no interest as an act of Christian charity. Let him remember that he has a contract with me and that he must not renege on it!"

"Why, I am sure, if he reneges on his contract," Salarino said, "you will not take a pound of his flesh. What would that be good for?"

"I could use it as bait for fish," Shylock replied. "If Antonio's flesh will feed nothing else, it will feed my revenge. He has acted badly toward me, and he has cost me half a million ducats in my business. He has laughed at my losses, mocked at my gains, scorned my Jewish nation, thwarted my business deals, cooled and alienated my friends, and heated my enemies to be even more against me.

"What is his reason for so treating me? His reason is that I am a Jew. Has not a Jew eyes? Has not a Jew hands, organs, limbs, senses, affections, passions? Are not Jews fed with the same food, hurt with the same weapons, subject to the same diseases, healed by the same means, warmed and cooled by the same winter and summer, as a Christian is? If you prick us, do we not bleed? If you tickle us, do we not laugh? If you poison us, do we not die? And if you wrong us, shall we not seek revenge? If we are like you in the rest, we will resemble you in that.

"If a Jew should wrong a Christian, what does the Christian do? Practice Christian humility? No. Get revenge? Yes. If a Christian should wrong a Jew, what should the Jew do according to the examples set by the Christians? Exercise forbearance? No. According to Christian examples, the Jew should seek revenge. The villany that you Christians teach me, I will practice, and I will do my best to improve on the examples and be more villainous than you Christians."

One of Antonio's servants arrived and said to Solanio and Salarino, "Gentlemen, my master, Antonio, is at his house and desires to speak with you both."

Salarino replied, "We have been up and down and all around seeking him."

Tubal, one of Shylock's Jewish friends, arrived.

Solanio said, "Here comes another of the tribe of Jews; a third Jew cannot be found who would match these two unless the Devil converts and becomes a Jew."

Solanio, Salarino, and Antonio's servant departed.

Shylock said, "How are you, Tubal! What news do you bring me from Genoa? Did you find my daughter?"

"I often heard news about her, but I could not find her," Tubal said.

"This is bad news indeed!" Shylock said. "I have lost so much wealth. One of the diamonds my daughter stole from me cost me two thousand ducats at the great annual jewel fair in Frankfort, Germany! The curse never fell upon our Jewish nation until now — at least, I never felt it until now. Daniel 9:11 says, *'Yea, all Israel have transgressed thy law, even by departing, that they might not obey thy voice; therefore the curse is poured upon us, and the oath that is written in the law of Moses the servant of God, because we have sinned against him.'* I lost two thousand ducats with the loss of that jewel, and my daughter also stole other precious, precious jewels.

"I wish that my daughter were dead and lying at my feet, and the jewels were in her earrings! I wish that she were lying at my feet in a coffin, and that my ducats were in the coffin!

"No news of them? Why, that's the way it is. I do not know how much I have spent in the search for my jewels and my ducats. I have suffered loss upon loss! The thief fled with so much of my wealth, and I have spent so much of my wealth to find the thief, and I have found no satisfaction, no revenge. The only ill luck I have seen is what falls upon my own shoulders. I hear no sighs except those that are formed by own breath. I see no tears but those that I have shed."

"Other men have ill luck, too," Tubal replied. "Antonio, as I heard in Genoa — "

"What? Antonio has had ill luck? What ill luck?"

"One of his merchant ships, one coming from Tripolis, wrecked."

"I thank God, I thank God. Is it true, is it true?"

Tubal replied, "I spoke with some of the sailors who escaped the shipwreck."

"I thank you, good Tubal. This is good news, good news! Where did you hear this news? In Genoa?"

"Your daughter spent in Genoa, so I heard, eighty ducats in one night."

"It is as if you have stuck a dagger in me," Shylock said. "I shall never see my gold again. My daughter spent fourscore ducats on a single occasion! Fourscore ducats!"

"Several of Antonio's creditors came with me as I traveled back to Venice. They swear that Antonio cannot avoid bankruptcy."

"I am very glad to hear it," Shylock said. "I'll plague him; I'll torture him. I am glad to hear that he will go bankrupt."

"One of Antonio's creditors showed me a ring that he had received from your daughter in a trade for a monkey."

"Damn!" Shylock said. "You are torturing me! That was my turquoise ring. Leah gave it to me when I was a bachelor. I would not have traded it for a wilderness of monkeys."

"But Antonio is certainly undone. He has no choice but to go bankrupt."

"That's true, that's very true," Shylock said. "Go, Tubal, find a police officer for me and give him the amount of money that he requires to arrest someone for nonpayment of debts. Engage the police officer a fortnight before Antonio is required to repay the money he borrowed from me. I will cut the heart out of him, if he forfeits. If Antonio is not around any longer, I can make whatever business deals I want to make and make whatever profit I want to make. Go, Tubal, and meet me at our synagogue. I need to make an oath. Go, good Tubal; meet me at our synagogue, Tubal."

Bassanio, Portia, Gratiano, Nerissa, and some attendants entered the room that contained the three caskets.

Portia was in love with Bassanio, but she wished to hide it and deny it.

She said to him, "Please, wait. Tarry a day or two before you guess which casket holds my picture because if you choose the wrong casket I will lose your company and will no longer see you. Therefore, wait a while before you choose a casket. There is something that tells me, but it is not love, that I do not want to lose your company. Take my advice. Hatred does not give this kind of advice; if I hated you, I would not give you this advice.

"But in case you should not understand me well — and yet a virgin has no tongue but thought, for it is said that maidens should be seen and not heard — I would detain you here one month or two before you choose a casket and try to win me as your wife. I could tell you which is the casket that contains my picture, but I have sworn not to do that and so I will not tell you. Because of that, you may choose the wrong casket and not marry me. If you do choose the wrong casket, you will make me wish a sin — you will make me wish that I had broken my oath and told you which casket to choose.

"Shame on your eyes because they have bewitched me and divided me. One half of me is yours, and the other half is also yours. I should say that the other half of me is mine, but what is mine is yours, and so it is also yours. These evil times put bars between the owners and their rights — they keep owners from claiming what is theirs!

"If it should happen that you choose the wrong casket and I am lost to you, let Fortune — not I — go to Hell for depriving you of what belongs to you. I speak too long, but I speak to drag out the time, to stretch it and to draw it out at length, in order to keep you from choosing a casket."

"Let me choose," Bassanio said. "The way I feel now, it is as if I am being tortured on the rack because I do not know whether you will be mine."

"Tortured on the rack, Bassanio!" Portia cried. "Traitors are tortured on the rack to force them to confess. Confess to me what treason is mingled with your love."

"The only treason is the ugly treason of mistrust," Bassanio said. "I am not certain that I will choose the right casket, and therefore I fear that I may not be able to marry you and enjoy having you as my wife. Snow and fire are as likely to be friends and live together as I am to be treasonous to you, my love."

"I am afraid of your words — afraid that you say them only because you are being tortured on the rack. Men who are being tortured on the rack will say anything."

"Promise me my life, and I'll confess the truth," Bassanio said.

"Well, then, confess and live," Portia said.

"To live is to love. 'Confess' and 'love' would have been my entire confession," Bassanio said. "I confess that I love you. This is a happy torment, when my torturer teaches me the answers that will set me free. But now allow me to choose a casket and see my fortune."

"Choose, then!" Portia said. "My picture is locked in one of the caskets. If you really love me, you will choose the casket with my picture. Such was the intention of my dying father when he designed this test, and good men have the gift of prophecy when they die.

"Nerissa and all the rest of you, stand a little distance away. Let music play while Bassanio makes his choice. Then, if he chooses the wrong casket, he will make a swan-like end — the swan sings its beautiful song only when it is dying — and vanish away with the music. That the comparison of the swan song and this music may be more proper, my eyes shall be the stream and the watery deathbed for him. If he chooses wrongly, I will cry and he shall drown in my tears.

"But he may choose the right casket, and what is the music then? Then the music is like the flourish of trumpets when true subjects bow before a new-crowned Monarch.

"The music will be like those dulcet sounds at break of day that creep into the dreaming bridegroom's ears, and summon him to go to church to be married. Now the bridegroom goes, with no less presence, but with much more love, than young Hercules, when he redeemed the virgin tribute paid by weeping Trojans to the sea-monster. Hesione, the sister of Priam, the future King of Troy, was chained to a rock on the shore so she would be sacrificed to the sea-monster, but Hercules killed the sea-monster and saved her life.

"I will stand here and represent Hesione, the sacrifice. The other women here can represent the Trojan wives, who, with tear-stained faces, came forth to witness the outcome of Hercules' intended rescue. Go, Hercules! If you continue to live and are not killed by the sea-monster, then I will continue to live. With much, much more dismay do I view the battle than you who are fighting in it."

Music played, and Portia sang this song:

"Tell me where is fancy bred,

"In the heart, or in the head?

"How begot, how nourished?"

The women in the room sang, *"Reply, reply."*

Portia continued to sing:

"It is engendered in the eyes,

"With gazing fed; and fancy dies

"In the cradle where it lies.

"Let us all ring fancy's knell

"I'll begin it — ding, dong, bell. "

The women in the room sang, *"Ding, dong, bell."*

The song was about "love" and love. "Love" — a superficial fancy — is foolish affection brought about only by the eyes. A man can see a pretty woman and fall in "love." A woman can see a handsome man and fall in "love." The song warned that this "love" dies quickly and that this "love" ought to die quickly. A deeper love is needed that will not quickly die. One can conclude that the deeper love is risky and that whoever wants true love must give and hazard all he — or she — has. Whoever wants it must go deeper than surface appearances.

Having listened to the song, Bassanio knew which casket to choose. His "torturer" had taught him the answer that would set him free.

Bassanio said quietly to himself, "Surface appearances may be much different from the truth that is within. The world is continually deceived by ornament and appearance.

"In law, what plea is so tainted and corrupt that it cannot, being seasoned with a gracious and eloquent voice, hide evil? It is like rotten food whose foulness is masked with spices.

"In religion, what damned error — heresy — exists that some sober brow will not bless it and approve it with a text quoted from the Bible and hide its grossness with a fair ornament?

"There is no vice so simple and uncomplicated that it cannot assume some mark of virtue on his outward parts.

"How many cowards, whose hearts are all as false as stairs or ropes made of sand, wear yet upon their chins the manly beards of Hercules and frowning Mars? Yet, these cowards lack the red blood of courage that Hercules and Mars have in abundance. They grow beards to look manly but lack manliness.

"Look on beauty, and you shall see that it is purchased by the ounce — both cosmetics and hair are bought by the ounce. These things work a miracle in nature — people who wear the most cosmetics and wear the most hair that did not grow on their head are the most morally dissolute. Those curled snaky golden locks that make such wanton and promiscuous gambols with the wind, those golden locks that appear to be so beautiful, are actually a gift from someone else's head, a head that is now in a sepulcher, a head whose hair was harvested to be sold.

"Therefore, ornament is the treacherous shore of a most dangerous sea. Ornament is the beauteous scarf that veils a 'beauty' who is not beautiful. Ornament is the appearance of 'truth' which cunning times display to entrap the wisest.

"Therefore, thou gaudy gold, I will have nothing to do with you. You are hard food for Midas, whom Apollo granted the wish that everything that he touched would turn to gold. After this wish was granted, Midas was no longer able to eat or drink.

"And I want nothing to do with you, silver, you pale and common drudge that is made into coins that pass from man to man.

"But you, you poor lead that threaten rather than promise anything, your paleness moves me more than eloquence. I choose the lead casket, and may joy be the consequence!"

Portia thought, *All my other emotions fly into the air and disappear. Gone are my doubtful thoughts, and rashly embraced despair, and shuddering fear, and green-eyed jealousy! Only love remains, and it is not moderate. Love, be moderate; lessen your ecstasy. Rein in your joy and make it moderate; reduce this excess. I feel too much your blessing: Make it less. I am afraid that I will grow ill and die from feeling too much happiness.*

Bassanio asked, "What will I find in here?"

He opened the lead casket and said, "I find Portia's picture! What artist — a demi-god! — has created a portrait so like the living person! Are the eyes in this portrait moving? Do they reflect the movement of my own eyes? Here are two lips that are parted with sugar breath. So sweet a barrier — her breath — has parted the sweet friends that are her lips. Here in her hair the painter has played the spider and has woven a golden mesh to entrap the hearts of men faster and more securely than gnats are caught in cobwebs. Her eyes — how could the artist see to paint them? After the artist had painted one of her eyes, I would think its beauty would have dazzled and blinded him and made him unable to paint her other eye. Still, as much as my praise falls short of what this portrait deserves, just as much does this painting fall short of capturing the beauty of the living woman depicted in it.

"Here is a scroll that will tell me my fortune. I will read it out loud:

"*You who choose not by looks and view,*

"*Choose fairly and choose truly!*

"*Since this fortune falls to you,*

"*Be content and seek no new fortune,*

"*If you are well pleased with this*

"*And accept this fortune as your bliss,*

"*Turn to where your lady is*

"*And claim her with a loving kiss.*

"This is a kind scroll. Fair lady, if I have your permission, I come by the authority of the scroll to give and receive a kiss. I am like one of two people contending for a prize, one who thinks he has done well in people's eyes, one who hears applause and general shouting, one who is giddy in spirit, but who is still gazing in doubt whether these pearls of praise be for him or not. Thus stand I, three times beautiful lady. I am as doubtful whether what I see is true, until it is confirmed, signed, and ratified by you."

"You see me, Lord Bassanio, where I stand — such as I am," Portia replied. "Though for myself alone, I would not be ambitious in my wish, to wish myself much better; yet, for you I would be trebled twenty times myself. For you, I would be a thousand times more beautiful, ten thousand times richer. Only so that you would value me highly, I wish that I could exceed all calculations in virtue, beauty, possessions, and friends. However, the full sum of me is a sum that can be calculated. What gross sum is that? I am an unlessoned girl; I am unschooled, unpracticed. It is fortunate that I am not so old that I cannot learn. Even more fortunate, I am not so dull but that I can learn. Most fortunate of all is that my gentle spirit commits itself to your spirit to be directed and educated; you will be my lord, my governor, my King.

"Because we are engaged to be married, I am now part of you, and what is mine is now yours. Just now I was the lord of this fair mansion, I was master of my servants, I was Queen over myself. But right now, this house, these servants and I myself are yours, my lord. I give them to you, and I give you this ring; if you ever part from, lose, or give away this ring, let it foretell the ruin and decay of your love and be my opportunity to denounce you."

Bassanio replied, "Madam, you have taken away all my words; I do not know what to say. Only my blood — my passion — speaks to you in my veins, and my mind suffers such confusion. It is like after a Prince has beautifully given a speech, and the multitude of hearers, all buzzing with pleasure, speak separately but their sentences and sounds all blend together in a hurrah of joy. When this ring that you have given me parts from this finger, then life will part from me. When I no longer wear this ring, then you may say boldly that I, Bassanio, am dead."

Nerissa said, "My lord and lady, it is now time for us, who have stood by and seen our wishes for your happiness be granted, to say to you, 'Good joy. Good joy, my lord and lady!'"

Bassanio's being engaged to marry a very rich woman greatly elevated his social status, something that Gratiano acknowledged in the way he referred to him: "My Lord Bassanio and my gentle lady, Portia, I wish you all the joy that you can wish because I am sure that you will not wish any of my joy away from me. When you two are married, I ask you, please, that at that time I may be married, too."

"I grant that with all my heart," Bassanio said, "provided that you can find someone to marry you."

"I thank you, your lordship, because you yourself have gotten me a woman who will marry me," Gratiano said. "My eyes, my lord, can look as swiftly as yours. You saw the mistress, Portia. I beheld the waiting-gentlewoman, Nerissa. You loved, and I loved. I wasted no time wooing Nerissa, just as you wasted no time wooing Portia. Your fortune stood upon the casket there, and so did mine, too, as it happened. I wooed Nerissa so hard that I was sweating, and I sweat so much that the roof of my mouth was dry because of the oaths of love I swore. At last, if her promise lasts and Nerissa keeps her promise to marry me, I will marry beautiful Nerissa, who said that she would give me her love and marry me, provided that you won and married her mistress, Portia."

Portia asked, "Is this true, Nerissa?"

"Madam, it is, as long as you approve."

"And do you, Gratiano, mean good faith?" Bassanio asked. "Do you have good intentions toward Nerissa?"

"Yes," Gratiano replied. "I swear it by my Christian faith, my lord."

"Our wedding feast shall be much honored by your marriage," Bassanio said.

Gratiano said to Nerissa, "Let's bet them a thousand ducats that we shall have a son before they do."

"Do you want to gather the stake of money now and put it down?" Nerissa asked.

"If my 'stake' always stays down and is never erect, we shall never win the bet," Gratiano said. "But, look, some people are coming here. Who are they? Lorenzo and his infidel, Jessica the Jew? What, and my old Venetian friend Salario?"

Lorenzo, Jessica, and Salario entered the room.

Bassanio said, "Lorenzo and Salario, you are welcome here, if I, in the newness of my household authority, have the power to welcome you. Sweet Portia, with your permission, I bid my true friends and countrymen welcome."

"So do I, my lord," Portia said. "They are entirely welcome here."

"I thank your honor," Lorenzo said. "I had not intended to have seen you here, but I met Salario along the way, and he entreated me, not allowing me to decline, to come here with him."

"That is true, my lord," Salario said. "And I have a good reason for it. Signior Antonio commends him to you. Signior Antonio praises Lorenzo highly."

Salario gave Bassanio a letter.

Bassanio said, "Before I open this letter, please tell me how my good friend Antonio is doing."

"He is not sick, my lord," Salario said, "unless it is mentally. He is not well, either, unless it is mentally. His letter there will tell you how he is doing."

Gratiano said, "Nerissa, welcome yonder stranger, Jessica the Jew." This was considerate of Gratiano.

He added, "Let's shake hands, Salario."

They shook hands, and Gratiano said to him, "How is that royal merchant, good Antonio, doing? I know he will be glad of the success of Bassanio and me. We are Jasons; each of us has won the golden fleece."

"You may have won the golden fleece, but I wish that you won a fleet of golden ships — the ships that Antonio has lost," Salario replied.

Portia said, "The content of the letter that you gave to Bassanio is bitter and cursed. The color is draining from Bassanio's cheeks. A dear friend of his must have died; nothing else in the world could so change the complexion of a normal and healthy and steadfast man. Bassanio grows worse and worse! Please, Bassanio, because we are almost married, I am already one with you. I am half yourself, and I must have half of anything that this letter brings you."

"Sweet Portia, in this letter I have read some of the most unpleasant words that ever appeared on paper! Gentle lady, when I first told you that I loved you, I freely and openly told you that all the wealth I had was in the gentlemanly blood that runs in my veins — my social class is that of a gentleman. What I said then is true, and yet, dear lady, you shall see that when I told you that my wealth was nothing, I was then bragging. I should then have told you that I was worth less than nothing; for, indeed, I have borrowed money from a dear friend, who borrowed money from his worst enemy in order to lend me the money I needed. Here is a letter, my lady. If the paper the words are written on is like the body of my friend, every word in it would be a gaping wound from which pours the blood that is needed to keep my friend alive.

"But is it true, Salario? Have all of Antonio's business ventures failed? What, was not even one of them successful? Antonio had ships sailing home from Tripolis, from Mexico and England, and from Lisbon, Barbary, and India. Didn't even one merchant ship escape the dreadful touch of rocks that sink merchant ships and ruin merchants?"

"Not even one, my lord," Salario replied. "Besides, it appears that even if Antonio had the money he needs to pay back the Jew, the Jew would not take it. Never did I know a creature that bears the shape of man be so keen and greedy to destroy a man. Shylock appeals to the Duke morning and night for what he calls justice, and he says that if the Venetian government fails to give him justice that it will not be safe for merchants to do business there. Twenty merchants, the Duke himself, and the most important Venetian nobles have all argued with him, but none can keep him from insisting on his malicious desire to get what

Antonio promised to give — a pound of Antonio's flesh — if he did not pay back on the due date the money that he had borrowed."

Jessica, Shylock's estranged daughter, said, "When I was with him, I heard him swear to Tubal and to Chus, his Jewish countrymen, that he would rather have Antonio's flesh than twenty times the value of the sum that Antonio owes him. I know, my lord, that if law, authority, and power do not stop my father, that it will go hard with poor Antonio."

Portia asked, "Is Antonio your dear friend who is thus in trouble?"

"Antonio is the dearest friend to me, the kindest man, the best-dispositioned and unwearied spirit in doing courtesies, and one in whom the ancient Roman virtue of honor more appears than in any man who draws breath in Italy," Bassanio replied.

"How much money does he owe the Jew?" Portia asked.

"He borrowed for me from the Jew three thousand ducats," Bassanio said.

"What, no more?" Portia, a very wealthy woman, said. "Pay him six thousand, and cancel the contract. If you have to, pay him double six thousand, or pay him triple that. Do that before a friend of this description shall lose a single hair through Bassanio's fault.

"Bassanio, first go with me to church and make me your wife, and then you shall sail away to Venice and go to your friend. Never shall you lie by my side with an unquiet soul. You shall have gold to pay this petty debt twenty times over: When it is paid, bring your true friend back here with you. My waiting-gentlewoman Nerissa and I will in the meantime live the way that virgins and widows do. Come, let's hurry to the church! You must go away from here on your wedding day. Bid your friends welcome, and show them a merry face. Since you are dearly bought, I will love you dearly. But let me now hear the letter of your friend."

Bassanio read the letter out loud:

"*Sweet Bassanio, my ships have all miscarried and sunk, my creditors are growing cruel, my assets are very low, and I have been unable to repay the Jew the money I owe him. Because of that, I now owe him a pound of my flesh. Since it is impossible that I continue to live after I pay him what I owe him, all debts are cleared and forgiven between you and me if I can see you when I die. Notwithstanding, do what it pleases you to do. If your friendship for me does not persuade you to come to see me die, don't let my letter persuade you.*"

"Bassanio, my love, finish your business here quickly and go to Venice!" Portia said.

"Since I have your permission to go away, I will leave quickly," Bassanio said, "but, until I come back again, no bed shall ever be guilty of my stay. I will not sleep until I return to you. No bed will hold me back, and no rest will separate us."

— 3.3 —

On a street in Venice stood Shylock, Salarino, Antonio, and a jailer.

Shylock said, "Jailer, keep a close watch on Antonio. Do not talk to me about mercy. This is the fool who lent out money free of interest. Jailer, watch him closely."

"Listen to me, good Shylock," Antonio said.

"We have a contract," Shylock said to Antonio. "It is a legal contract, and I have sworn an oath that I will enforce it. You called me a dog before you had a reason to call me that. Therefore, since I am a dog, beware my fangs: The Duke shall grant me justice."

Shylock then said, "I do wonder, you wicked jailer, why you are so foolish that you appear outside the jail with Antonio just because he asked you to."

"Please, listen to me," Antonio said to Shylock.

"I will enforce the contract that you signed," Shylock said to Antonio. "I will not listen to you speak. We have a legal contract, so therefore stop your begging. I will not be made a soft and dull-eyed, easily manipulated fool. I will not nod in agreement with what you plead, will not relent, and will not sigh, and I will not yield to Christian pleaders on your behalf. Do not follow me. I want to hear no pleading. I do want the enforcement of our contract."

Shylock angrily exited.

Salarino said, "He is the most hard-hearted cur that has ever lived among men."

"Let him alone," Antonio said. "I will follow him no more and plead for a mercy that he will not grant me. He seeks my life, and I well know the reason why. I have often helped people who complained to me that they could not repay money they owed to him, and so Shylock did not profit by the forfeiture of their contracts. That is why Shylock hates me."

"I am sure that the Duke will never allow Shylock to take a pound of your flesh," Salarino said.

"The Duke cannot deny the course of law," Antonio said. "Merchants who trade here but are not citizens of Venice rely on the law to protect their interests. If the Duke does not enforce the law in my case, it will affect negatively the business interests and prosperity of Venice because people of all nations do so much trade and business here. Therefore, let us go. These griefs and losses of mine have made me lose so much weight that I shall hardly spare the pound of flesh I must give tomorrow to my bloodthirsty creditor.

"Well, jailer, let us go on. I pray to God that Bassanio shall come to see me pay his debt. If that happens, then I do not care what else happens!"

— 3.4 —

In a room in Portia's house in Belmont, she, Nerissa, Lorenzo, and Jessica were talking. Balthasar, who was one of her servants, was also present.

Lorenzo said to Portia, "Madam, although I say it in your presence, you have a noble and true conception of godlike friendship, as you have shown very strongly in bearing thus the absence of Bassanio, your lord and husband. But if you knew Antonio, to whom you show this honor and send relief, and how true a gentleman he is and how dear a friend to my lord your husband, I know you would be prouder of this good deed than of ordinary acts of goodness."

Portia replied, "I have never repented the doing of good deeds, and I shall not repent this good deed I do now. Bassanio and Antonio are two companions who talk together and spend time together. They are souls who equally share friendship for each other, and in such cases the two friends equally share features, character, and spirit. That makes me think that this Antonio, because he is the bosom friend of my lord, must be like my lord. If that is true, how little is the money I have given to Bassanio to save the life of a person who is the likeness of my soul.

"A genuine friend is like a second self. Antonio is the genuine friend of Bassanio, and so Antonio is the second self of Bassanio. I am one with Bassanio, and so Antonio is the second self of me and therefore he is the likeness of my soul. I have given money to save the semblance of my soul from a state of Hellish misery! By saving Antonio, I am saving myself, and therefore I do not want to hear praise of my 'good deed' — a 'good deed' in which I save myself. Therefore, speak no more about it.

"Lorenzo, I now commit into your hands the care and management of my house until my lord and husband's return. As for me, I have made a secret vow toward Heaven to live in prayer and contemplation, attended only by Nerissa here, until her husband and my husband return. A monastery is located two miles away from here, and there we will reside until our husbands return. I ask you not to deny my request that necessity and my friendship for you require me to ask of you."

"Madam, with all my heart I shall obey you and your fair commands."

"I have already informed my servants that you will take over for a while, and they will obey the orders of you and Jessica until Lord Bassanio and I return. And so farewell, until we shall meet again."

"May fair thoughts and happy hours attend on you!" Lorenzo said.

"I wish your ladyship all your heart's content," Jessica said.

"I thank you for your wish, and I wish you the same thing," Portia said. "May you fare well, Jessica."

Jessica and Lorenzo left the room.

Portia said, "Now, Balthasar, I have always found you to be honest and trustworthy, and I hope that now I may find that you have not changed. Take this letter and go as fast as a man can go to Padua, at whose university civil law is studied. Give my letter to my kinsman, Doctor Bellario, who is a doctor of law. Take whatever legal notes and lawyer's garments he gives to you as quickly as you can to the public ferry that travels to and from Venice. Waste no time in words, but leave immediately. I will be at the ferry before you get there."

"Madam, I go with all appropriate speed," Balthasar said.

He departed to perform his task.

Portia said, "Come, Nerissa, I have work in hand that you do not yet know about. We'll see our husbands before they shall even miss us."

"Shall our husbands see us?" Nerissa asked.

Portia answered, "They shall see us, Nerissa, but we will be wearing male clothing and so they shall think that we possess the male appendage that we lack.

"I will bet you that when we are both wearing male clothing that I will be the more masculine. I will carry my dagger with the finer grace, and speak between the change of man and boy with a high-pitched voice, and I will turn two of my usual small steps into one manly stride, and I will speak about fights like a fine bragging youth, and I will tell quaint lies about what ladies have between their legs and about how honorable ladies have sought my love, which

I denied them, and so they fell sick and died. I could not keep them from dying — because I lack the necessary equipment to requite their love. I will feel sorry that they died because of their love for me, and I will wish that I had not killed them. I will tell twenty of these puny and feeble lies, and men will think that I have been out of school for a year and so I am a real man. I have memorized a thousand crude tricks and lies used by these bragging Jacks, and I will use them when I am disguised as a young man."

"Why, shall we turn to men?" Nerissa said.

"Good Heavens, what kind of a question is that?" Portia said. "If you were overheard by a lewd interpreter, he would think that you are talking about turning over in bed so that you are facing a man! But come, I'll tell you all about my plan while we are travelling in my coach, which is waiting for us at the park gate. Therefore, let us make haste and go away because we must travel twenty miles today."

— 3.5 —

In a corner of the garden of Portia's house, Launcelet the jester and Jessica the Jew were talking.

"Yes, I truly believe that you are damned," Launcelet said, "because, you see, the sins of the father are to be laid upon the children: therefore, I promise you that I am afraid that you are damned. I have always plainly spoken my mind to you, and so now I speak to you my agitated cogitation of the matter. Therefore, be of good cheer because truly I think you are damned. There is only one hope in this situation that can do you any good; and that is only a kind of bastard hope."

"Please tell me what hope is that."

"You may hope that your father did not beget you, that you are not Shylock the Jew's daughter."

"That is a kind of bastard hope, indeed," Jessica said. "I would be a bastard indeed, but in that case, the sins of my mother would be visited upon me. The child of a Jewish woman is a Jew."

"In that case," Launcelet said, "truly I fear you are damned both by father and mother. When I shun Scylla, your father, I fall into Charybdis, your mother. Scylla was a monster, and Charybdis was a whirlpool. In Homer's *Odyssey*, Odysseus had to sail between them."

Launcelot thought, *I fall into Charybdis, your mother. That can mean, I fall into your mother's hole. Yes, I just made an I-slept-with-yo'-momma joke.*

Launcelot concluded, "Well, you are damned and gone to Hell either way."

Jessica said, "I shall be saved by my husband; he has made me a Christian. Remember 1 Corinthians 7:14: *"For the unbelieving husband is sanctified by the wife, and the unbelieving wife is sanctified by the husband: else were your children unclean; but now are they holy."*

"In that case, your husband is the more to blame," Launcelot said. "We Christians were numerous enough before. Fortunately, we were not so numerous that we could not live peacefully next to each other. But this making of more Christians will make the price of hogs rise. Jews do not eat pork and bacon. If they convert and begin to eat meat from pigs, soon bacon will be so expensive that no one will be able to buy it."

"Launcelot, I will tell my husband, Lorenzo, what you said. Here he comes."

Lorenzo said, "I shall grow jealous of you soon, Launcelot, if you keep getting my wife into corners."

Jessica said, "No, you need not fear us doing anything immoral, Lorenzo. Launcelot and I are arguing. He tells me flatly that there is no mercy for me in Heaven because I am a Jew's daughter, and he says that you are not a good member of society because by converting Jews to Christians, you raise the price of pork."

"I can defend myself from the charge you make against me, Launcelot, better than you can defend yourself from the charge of making the belly of Portia's black servant swell up," Lorenzo said. "The Moor is with child by you, Launcelot."

"It is much that the Moor should be more — bigger — than reasonable," Launcelot said, "but even if she is less than a chaste woman, she is still more than I took her to be."

Launcelot thought, *Yes, she is more than when I took her. I took her sexually, and now her womb is populated.*

Lorenzo said, "How every fool can play upon words and commit wordplay! Puns, puns, and more puns! I think the best wit will soon be silence, and only parrots will be praised for talking. Go inside, Launcelot, and tell the servants to prepare for dinner."

"The servants are prepared for dinner," Launcelot said. "All of them are hungry and have good appetites."

"Good God!" Lorenzo said. "What a wit-cracker you are! Then tell the servants to prepare dinner."

"That is done, too, sir," Launcelot replied, "but 'cover' is the right word. The table must be covered with a tablecloth for dinner, and the food must be put in covered dishes so it can be brought to the table."

"In that case, then 'cover' is the word I use, Launcelet."

"Cover my head with a hat, sir!" Launcelot said. "Not I. I know that servants are supposed to be bareheaded when with their superiors, sir!"

"Still more punning no matter what the topic of conversation is!" Lorenzo complained. "Are you going to show off the whole wealth of your wit on one occasion? Won't you save some of your wit for later? Please, understand a plain man who is speaking plainly. Go to your fellow servants, tell them to get the table ready so that we can eat and to put the food on the table, and then we will come in to dinner."

"The table shall be gotten ready, the food will be served in covered dishes, and as for your coming in to dinner, sir, why, do whatever your own inclinations and whims would have you do."

Launcelot exited. Jessica had been much more amused by Launcelot's jesting than Lorenzo had been.

"Such sagacity!" Lorenzo said, sarcastically. "Launcelot's words suit him — he is a fool and he talks like a fool. Launcelot the fool has planted in his memory an army of good words that he can use to pun with. I know many fools who have better positions than his and wear the same kind of jester's costume, who constantly play tricks with words and make nonsense of whatever sense the person they talk to tries to make.

"But how are you, Jessica? And, good and sweet Jessica, tell me what you think about Portia. Do you like the Lord Bassanio's wife?"

"I like her more than I can say," Jessica said. "The Lord Bassanio really needs to live a morally upright life because, having such a blessing in his wife, he finds the joys of Heaven here on Earth. If he does not act here on Earth to merit such a blessing, then it stands to reason that he should never get to Heaven. Why, if two gods were to play some Heavenly game and each bet an Earthly woman on the outcome, and Portia were one of those women, then the other god must wager a woman and something more in order to make the prizes fair and equal because no woman here in this poor rude world is the equal of Portia. She is better than any other woman."

"As worthy a wife she is to Bassanio, just as worthy am I a husband to you," Lorenzo said in a gentle, joking tone of voice.

"You need to ask me for my opinion about that," Jessica replied, also in a gentle, joking tone of voice.

"I will, and soon," Lorenzo said. "First, let us go in to dinner."

"Not yet," Jessica said, "let me praise you while I have a stomach — both an appetite and the inclination — to praise you."

"Please, let this serve for table conversation as we eat," Lorenzo said. "Whatever you say, I will digest your words — among other things."

"Well, I'll set you forth," Jessica said. "I will set you at the table, and I will give you large servings of praise."

CHAPTER 4

— 4.1 —

The Duke and the Magnificoes — the Magnates — of Venice — entered the courtroom, and then, using a different door, Antonio, Bassanio, Gratiano, Salario, and others entered the courtroom.

The Duke asked, "Is Antonio here?"

Antonio replied, "I am present, so please your grace."

"I am sorry for you," the Duke said to him. "You have come to answer a stony adversary, an inhuman wretch who is incapable of pity and who is void and empty of even a tiny quantity of mercy."

Antonio replied, "I have heard that your grace has taken great pains to moderate Shylock's rigorous course; but since he stands obdurate, firm, and resolute and since no lawful means can carry me out of the reach of his envy, I do match my patience and endurance of pain against his fury, and I am prepared to endure, with a quietness of spirit, the great cruelty and rage of his spirit."

The Duke, "One of you, go and call the Jew into the court."

Salario answered, "He is ready and waiting at the door; here he comes, my Lord."

Carrying a sharp knife and a pair of scales, Shylock entered the courtroom, and the Duke said to the others present, "Make room, and let him stand before me."

The Duke then said, "Shylock, the world thinks, and I think so, too, that you are intending to put on an act of malice and evil until the last moment, and then it is thought that you shall show your mercy and pity — a mercy and pity that are stranger and more extraordinary than is your strange and extraordinary pretense of cruelty.

"We think that although now you insist on collecting the penalty for the forfeiture of poor Antonio's debt, which is one pound of his flesh, that you will not only not insist on collecting the pound of flesh but that you, touched with human gentleness and love, will also forgive a part of the principal that was borrowed so that it need not be paid back.

60

"We think that you will do these things because you will look with an eye of pity on Antonio's losses that have recently and heavily piled on his back. His losses have been large enough to bankrupt a merchant who has had very substantial wealth. His losses have also been large enough to make merciful the stony and flinty and hard hearts of stubborn, cruel, and bloodthirsty Turks and Tartars, who have not been educated to show tender courtesy to others.

"We all expect a gentle and merciful answer befitting a gentleman from you, Jew."

Shylock replied, "I have informed your grace about what I want, and I have sworn by our holy Sabbath to have the pound of Antonio's flesh that is called for, according to my contract with him. If you deny me that pound of flesh, then Jewish and foreign merchants who, like me, are not citizens of Venice, will doubt whether the laws of Venice will protect their rights and freedom. If that happens, then Venice will suffer financially. Therefore, you must enforce the legal contract that Antonio and I have made.

"You must want to ask me why I rather choose to have a pound of carrion flesh than to receive the three thousand ducats that Antonio owes me. I will not answer that except to say that it is my whim to take a pound of Antonio's flesh — I simply feel like taking a pound of his flesh instead of three thousand ducats. Does that answer your question? Suppose that a rat troubles my house, and I am willing to pay ten thousand ducats to have it poisoned. Does that answer your question? Some men do not like seeing a roast pig with its mouth open on the banquet table. Some men become insane when they see a cat. Other men, when they hear the nasal tone of a bagpipe, hate it so much that they pee themselves. People like or dislike things according to desires that they have by nature and that affect how strongly they feel about their likes and dislikes.

"Now, as for the answer to your question, just as there is no obviously right answer to the questions of why one man hates a roast pig with an open mouth, why a second man hates a harmless and useful cat, and why a third man hates a bagpipe wrapped in cloth, but are forced involuntarily by their nature to act on their hatred although doing so offends other people, I can give you no reason for why I want a pound of Antonio's flesh other than to say that I deeply hate and loathe Antonio so much that I prefer to take a pound of his flesh rather than the three thousand ducats he owes me. Does that answer your question?"

"This is not an answer, you unfeeling man, that will excuse the outpouring of your cruelty," Bassanio said, although Shylock had been addressing the Duke.

"I am not obligated to please you with my answers," Shylock said to Bassanio.

"Do all men kill the living things they do not love?" Bassanio asked.

Shylock replied, "Does any man hate a living thing that he would not kill?"

"Not every displeasure is a hate at first," Bassanio said.

Shylock replied, "Would you allow a snake to bite you twice?"

"Please, remember that you are arguing with Shylock the Jew," Antonio said. "You may as well go stand upon the beach and tell the ocean not to have a high tide. You may as well argue with a wolf about why the wolf made a ewe bleat for her lamb. You may as well forbid the mountain pines to wag their high tops and to make noise when the gusts of the skies blow against them. You may as well do anything that is the most difficult rather than try to soften Shylock's Jewish heart — is anything harder than that? Therefore, I ask you to try to make no more bargains with and arguments opposing Shylock. Instead, quickly and plainly let me know the judgment of the court — the Jew will have what he wants."

Bassanio ignored Antonio's request and said to Shylock, "Antonio owes you three thousand ducats, but I will pay you six thousand ducats."

Shylock replied, "If each of the six thousand ducats were divided into six parts and each part became a full ducat, I would not take them. I insist on taking a pound of Antonio's flesh."

The Duke asked Shylock, "How can you ever hope for mercy since you yourself show no mercy? Don't you fear a merciless judgment being made against you?"

"What judgment shall I fear, since I am doing no wrong?" Shylock replied. "You Christians have among you many slaves whom you have purchased. You treat these slaves like you treat your asses and your dogs and your mules; you treat them abjectly and work them hard — you own them. Shall I say to you, 'Let your slaves be free, and let them marry your children and inherit your wealth. Why should your slaves sweat as they work for you? Let your slaves' beds be as soft as your beds and let their food be the same kind of food that you eat'? You will answer, 'The slaves are ours to treat as we wish.'

"I answer you the way that you will answer me: The pound of flesh that I am demanding from Antonio is dearly bought. I paid for it, it is mine, and I will have it.

"If you deny me, then your laws mean nothing! If you break the laws of Venice, then the law will have no force. I want my legal contract with Antonio to be enforced by the laws of Venice. I want justice. Tell me, shall I receive it?"

The Duke replied, "I have the power to dismiss this court unless Bellario, a learned doctor of civil law in Padua, whom I have asked to come here to judge this case, comes here today."

Salario said, "My lord, outside this courtroom is a messenger with a letter from the doctor; the messenger has just now come from Padua."

The Duke ordered, "Bring us the letter; tell the messenger to come and stand here in front of me."

Bassanio said, "Be of good cheer, Antonio! What, man, have courage! Shylock the Jew shall have my flesh, blood, bones, and everything else before you shall lose for me even one drop of blood."

"I am a sick and contaminated wether — a castrated ram," Antonio said. "I am most suitable for death. The weakest kind of fruit drops earliest to the ground, and so let me die. You can best employ your time, Bassanio, in staying alive and writing my epitaph."

Nerissa, dressed like a lawyer's young clerk, entered the courtroom, carrying a letter.

"Have you come from Padua, from Bellario?" the Duke asked.

"I have come from both, my lord," Nerissa said. "Bellario greets your grace."

She gave the Duke the letter.

As the Duke read the letter, Shylock began to whet — to sharpen — his knife on the leather sole of one of his shoes.

Bassanio asked him, "Why are you sharpening your knife so eagerly?"

"I am getting ready to cut off a pound of flesh from that bankrupt there," Shylock replied.

"Not on your sole, but on your soul, harsh Jew," Gratiano said, "are you sharpening your knife, but no metal — not even the metal of the executioner's axe — can possess half the keenness of your sharp malice. Can no prayers penetrate your heart and persuade you to be merciful?"

"No, none," Shylock said. "None that you are able to make."

Gratiano said, "Be damned, you dog! It is impossible to hate you as much as you deserve to be hated. People must wonder whether justice exists when they see that you are alive. You almost make me waver in my Christian faith and believe in Pythagoras' heretical theory of the transmigration of souls. He believed that the soul of an animal could appear in the body of a man. Your spirit is doglike; your spirit may have been that of a wolf that killed a man, was found guilty, and therefore was hung and killed. In our society, we sometimes put on trial and punish animals. From the gallows the wolf's murderous spirit flew and while you were in the womb of your unholy and non-Christian mother, it infused itself in you. Your desires are those of wolves — your desires are bloody, starved, and ravenous."

"Unless you can shout the seal off the legal contract that Antonio and I signed," Shylock said, "you are hurting only your own lungs by speaking so loudly. Start using your brain, good youth, or it will be completely and permanently ruined through lack of use. I am here in this court to get justice, not to listen to you."

Having finished reading the letter, the Duke said, "This letter from Bellario praises a young and learned doctor and recommends that he appear as judge in our court. Where is he?"

Nerissa said, "He is waiting outside, near here, to find out whether or not you will allow him to enter the courtroom."

"He can enter here with all my heart," the Duke said. "Some three or four of you go and give him courteous conduct to this place. Meanwhile, the court shall hear Bellario's letter."

Three or four attendants departed.

The Duke read out loud,

"Your grace should know that when I received your letter to me that I was very sick, but when your messenger came with your letter, a young doctor of Rome, whose name is Balthasar, was visiting me as a friend. I informed him about the case between Shylock the Jew and Antonio the merchant. We consulted many books together. I have told Balthazar my opinion of the case. My opinion, which has been supplemented by and bettered by Balthazar's own learning, the greatness whereof I cannot enough praise, comes with him, at my request, to fulfill your grace's request for legal expertise since I am too ill to travel. Please, do not think lowly of Balthazar because of his youth, for I never knew so young a body to have

so old — that is, so wise — a head. I trust that you will graciously accept his help. His performance at the trial will be so impressive and expert that it will greatly increase his reputation."

The Duke said, "You have heard what the learned Bellario wrote to me."

He looked up, saw Portia, dressed like a lawyer, entering the courtroom, and said, "And here, I take it, is Balthazar, the young doctor of civil law."

The Duke said, "Shake hands with me."

They shook hands. The Duke asked, "Have you come from old Bellario?"

"I have, my lord."

"You are welcome. Prepare to judge this case. Are you acquainted with the dispute that is being judged in this courtroom?"

"I am thoroughly informed about the dispute," Portia said. "Who is the merchant here, and who is the Jew?"

"Antonio and old Shylock, both of you step forward," the Duke said.

They did.

Portia asked, "Is your name Shylock?"

"Shylock is my name."

Portia said to him, "This lawsuit of yours is unusual, yet the law of Venice cannot stop you from pursuing it."

She then said to Antonio, "You are in debt to Shylock, and so he has power over you — is that right?"

"Yes, I am in debt to him, and he says that he has power over me."

"Do you confess that you owe him money?"

"I do."

"Then the Jew must be merciful and not take a pound of your flesh," Portia said.

"Are you forcing me to be merciful?" Shylock said. "How do you justify that? Why should I be constrained to be merciful?"

"The quality of mercy cannot be constrained — mercy cannot be forced," Portia said. "Mercy drops as the gentle rain drops from Heaven upon the place beneath it. Mercy blesses twice: It blesses the person who gives mercy, and it blesses the person who receives mercy.

"Mercy is mightiest in the mightiest: mercy is the most powerful quality of the most powerful people. Mercy becomes the Monarch on his throne more than his crown becomes him. The Monarch's scepter shows the force of temporal power, the visible symbol of awe and majesty. Because of Kings' temporal power, people dread and fear them.

"But mercy is above this temporal power; mercy is enthroned in the hearts of Kings. Mercy is an attribute of God Himself. Earthly power shows itself to be like God's power when Earthly justice is tempered with mercy.

"Therefore, Jew, although you plead for justice, consider this: If justice were strictly enforced, none of us would ever see Heaven. None of us would ever be saved from damnation. All of us are guilty of sin. Therefore, we pray that God will show mercy to us. Remember the Lord's Prayer: In Matthew 6:12, Jesus prayed to God, his Father, '*And forgive us our debts, as we forgive our debtors.*' The Lord's Prayer teaches all of us to be merciful — to engage in deeds of mercy. I have spoken all of this in hopes that you will show mercy and not insist on strict justice. But if you do insist on strict justice, this strict Venetian court of law must pronounce a sentence against Antonio, this merchant here."

Shylock replied, "May my deeds fall upon my head. I will be responsible for what I am doing. I insist on a strict justice. I want the contract to be strictly enforced. I want a pound of Antonio's flesh."

"Isn't Antonio able to pay back the money he owes to you?" Portia asked.

Bassanio said, "Yes, here in this court I have the money that Antonio owes Shylock. I have twice the amount of money that Antonio owes Shylock, and I am willing to give Shylock that amount to repay the debt owed to him. If twice the amount owed is not enough, then I will legally bind myself to pay back ten times as much money as is owed him. I will bind myself to do that with the penalty for forfeiture being my hands, my head, and my heart. If ten times the amount owed is still not sufficient, then it must be the case that evil conquers righteousness. I beg you, Balthazar, use your authority to twist the law on this occasion: To do a great right, do a little wrong, and thwart the will of this cruel Devil."

"Twisting and misinterpreting the law must not happen," Portia replied. "No power in Venice can alter an established and decreed law. Twisting and misinterpreting the law will set a precedent, and that precedent will result in much evil in the future. Therefore, twisting and misinterpreting the law must not happen."

Shylock said, "This is a Daniel come to judge this case! Yes, a Daniel! Wise young judge, I honor you!"

In the very short Book of Susanna (considered part of the Apocrypha by some religious traditions; other religious traditions include it as chapter 13 of the Book of Daniel), two old men spied on a young woman named Susanna as she bathed alone in her garden. Afterward, they told her that unless she slept with them they would lie and say that she had been having sex with a young man. She refused to sleep with them, and they spread the lie. She was put on trial for promiscuity; if found guilty, she would be executed. Daniel talked to the two old men separately. Their stories were inconsistent, and Daniel was able to show that they were lying. Susanna went free, and the two old men were executed.

"Please let me see the contract," Portia requested.

Shylock gave it to her, saying, "Here it is, most reverend doctor, here it is."

Portia looked at Bassanio, who had offered Shylock twice the amount that he was owed. Of course, it was Portia's money, and she was willing to give three times the amount owed — or more — to save the life of Antonio, her husband's best friend.

She said, "Shylock, you have been offered three times the amount of money you are owed if you will stop this lawsuit and stop insisting on receiving a pound of Antonio's flesh."

Shylock replied, "An oath! An oath! I have made an oath to Heaven that I will have a pound of Antonio's flesh. Shall my soul be found guilty of perjury? No, I will not allow that to happen, not even if I were to receive as payment all of Venice."

"Truly, this contract has been breached by Antonio," Portia said. "According to the law, Shylock may claim a pound of flesh, to be by him cut off nearest Antonio the merchant's heart. But, Shylock, I urge you to be merciful. Take three times the amount of money that is owed to you, and let me tear up this contract."

"You may tear it up after I have received my pound of flesh," Shylock replied. "The debt must be paid according to the tenor of the law — according to the wording that is in the contract. It appears that you are a worthy judge. You know the law; your exposition of the law has been very sound. I charge you by the law, whereof you are a well-deserving pillar, to proceed and make your judgment. By my soul, I swear that the tongue of no man has the power to persuade me to change my mind. I will have a pound of Antonio's flesh because he forfeited on his contract."

Antonio said, "Most heartily do I ask the court to give its judgment in this case."

"Why, then, this is the court's judgment," Portia said. "You must prepare your chest to be cut into by his knife."

Happy, Shylock said, "You are a noble judge! You are an excellent young man!"

"The intent and purpose of the law is to uphold legal contracts, including the penalties that appear in those legal contracts, including the penalty in this one," Portia said.

"That is very true," Shylock said. "You are a wise and upright judge! You are much more mature than your youthful appearance suggests!"

Portia said to Antonio, "Open your shirt and lay bare your chest."

"Yes, his chest," Shylock said. "That is what the contract says, isn't that so, noble judge? The contract includes these words: 'nearest his heart.'"

"That is true," Portia said. "Is there a set of scales here to weigh the flesh?"

"I have them ready," Shylock replied.

"Have a surgeon stand by, Shylock, at your expense," Portia requested, "to stop the bleeding from his wounds, lest he bleed to death."

"Does the contract state that?" Shylock asked, knowing that it did not.

"The contract does not state that," Portia said, "but so what? It would be good if you did that much out of charity."

Shylock glanced at a copy of the contract and said, "I do not see that the presence of a surgeon is specified in the contract."

Portia asked Antonio, "You, merchant, have you anything to say?"

"Just a little," Antonio replied. "I am fortified in spirit and well prepared. Let us shake hands, Bassanio. Fare you well! Don't grieve because I am suffering this for you because in this Fortune shows herself to be kinder than is her custom. Fortune usually allows a man to outlive his wealth, to view with hollow eyes and a wrinkled brow a wretched old age of poverty. From that lingering punishment of much misery, Fortune has cut me off; I die before I can endure it. Commend me to your honorable wife. Tell her how I, Antonio, died. Say how I respected you and regarded you as a friend; speak well of me after I die. And, when the tale is told, ask her to judge whether or not Bassanio once had a true friend. Regret only that you shall lose your friend. If you do so, I will not regret paying your debt. Indeed, if the Jew cuts me deeply enough, I will repay the debt immediately with all my heart."

Bassanio replied, "Antonio, I am married to a wife who is as dear to me as life itself, but life itself, my wife, and all the world are not by me esteemed above your life. I would lose all — yes, I would sacrifice my life, my wife, and all the world — to this Devil, to deliver you from him and so save your life."

Hiding her mouth briefly with her hand, Portia smiled and thought, *Your wife would give you little thanks for that, if she were nearby and heard you say this to your friend.*

Gratiano said, "I have a wife, whom I love, but I wish that she were dead and in Heaven, so she could entreat some Heavenly power to change the mind of this currish Jew."

Hiding her mouth briefly with her hand, Nerissa smiled and thought, *It is well that you say this behind your wife's back, otherwise your wife would make your house unquiet.*

Shylock did not smile and thought, *These husbands are Christians. I have a daughter. I wish that any of the descendants of the Jew Barrabas, the thief who was saved from execution rather than Jesus, were her husband rather than a Christian!*

Shylock said out loud, "We are wasting time with trivialities. Please, let us get on with the sentence."

Portia said, "A pound of Antonio the merchant's flesh belongs to you. The court awards it, and the law requires that it be given to you."

"Most rightful judge!" Shylock said.

"And you must cut this flesh from off his chest," Portia said. "The law allows it, and the court awards it."

"Most learned judge!" Shylock said. "This is the sentence I wanted! Come, Antonio, prepare your chest!"

"Wait a minute," Portia said. "There is something else."

She had given Shylock ample opportunity to be merciful and still make a large profit. He could have received three times the money owed him if only he had agreed not to take a pound of Antonio's flesh. Shylock had even refused to pay a surgeon to stop Antonio's bleeding and so perhaps save his life.

Now Portia gave Shylock the sentence he deserved, not the sentence he wanted: "This contract entitles you to not even one drop of blood. The words expressly are 'a pound of flesh.' Go, and take your pound of flesh, but as you cut it from Antonio's body, if you shed even one drop of Christian blood, your lands and possessions, by the laws of Venice, become the property of the government of Venice."

Gratiano now praised Portia, using Shylock's language: "You are an upright judge! Look at him, Jew, and you will see a learned judge!"

Shylock asked, "Is that the law?"

"Yes, it is," Portia said. "You yourself shall see the act in writing. You wanted strict justice, and you shall have strict justice, although you will not now want it."

Gratiano said, "This is a learned judge! Look at him, Jew! He is a learned judge!"

"I accept this offer, then," Shylock said. "Pay me three times the amount of money owed to me, and I shall let the Christian go free."

Bassanio said, "Here is the money."

"Wait!" Portia said. "The Jew shall have all justice and all strict justice. Do not be hasty here. The Jew shall have nothing but the penalty that is stated in the contract."

Gratiano said, "Oh, Jew! Look at this upright judge, this learned judge!"

Portia said to Shylock, "Therefore prepare to cut off a pound of his flesh. Do not shed any blood, and do not cut off less or more than exactly a pound of flesh. If you cut off more or less than an exact pound, be it but only so much as a twentieth of a gram too much or too little — or even so much as makes the scales differ as much as the width of a hair — then you will be executed and all your wealth and possessions will become the property of the government of Venice."

Gratiano exclaimed, "A second Daniel! He is a Daniel, Jew! Now, infidel, I have you on the hip like a wrestler and I am ready to throw you."

"Jew, why are you pausing?" Portia asked. "Take your pound of flesh."

"Give me my principal, and let me go. Return to me the amount of money that was borrowed. No interest. No more than the principal only."

Bassanio said, "I have it ready for you; here it is."

"No," Portia said. "Shylock has refused the money here in the open court. He shall have strict justice according to what is stated in his contract."

"A Daniel — still I say it, a second Daniel!" Gratiano said. "I thank you, Jew, for teaching me that word."

"Shall I not even have my principal back?" Shylock said.

Portia replied, "You shall have nothing but the forfeiture that is described in the contract, and that to be taken by you at your peril, Jew."

"Why, then let the Devil allow Antonio to enjoy the money," Shylock said. "I'll stay here no longer to argue the case."

"Stay, Jew," Portia said. "The law has another hold on you. It is enacted in the laws of Venice, that if it be proved against an alien — and Jews are aliens and outsiders; they are not citizens of Venice — that by direct or indirect attempts he seeks the life of any citizen, the party against whom he plots shall seize one half of his wealth and property; the other half will be seized and go into the personal treasury of the Duke of Venice. In addition, the offender's life lies at the mercy of the Duke of Venice and no one else. I say that his law applies to you because it appears, by what has happened here in this court, that indirectly — and directly, too — you have contrived to take the life of the defendant; therefore, you have incurred the punishments that I have mentioned. And so, Shylock, get down on your knees and beg the Duke to be merciful."

Gratiano said to Shylock, "Beg for permission to hang yourself. However, since your wealth has been forfeited to the Venetian government, you do not have enough money left to buy a rope. Therefore, you will have to be hanged at the government's expense."

"Shylock, so that you shall see the difference of our spirits," the Duke said, "I pardon your life before you ask me for permission to continue to live. Half of your wealth now belongs to Antonio; the other half goes to the government of Venice, but if you show humility I can reduce that to a fine."

Portia said, "Yes, you can accept a fine rather than the half of the Jew's wealth that goes to the government of Venice, but what is Antonio's is Antonio's."

"No," Shylock said. "Don't pardon me. Take my life since you are taking everything else. You take my house when you take what props up and sustains my house; you take my life when you take away the means by which I live. I make my living through the lending of money at interest; if I have no money, I have no way of making a living."

Portia asked, "What mercy can you render to Shylock, Antonio?"

Gratiano said, "Give him a noose for free so that he can hang himself. Don't give him anything else, for God's sake."

Antonio replied to Portia, "If it pleases my lord the Duke and all the members of this court of law to levy the fine instead of taking one half of Shylock's wealth, I am content, as long as he will let me have the other half of his wealth to invest during his life, and then to give it, upon his death, to Lorenzo, the gentleman who recently stole away with and married his daughter. I do have two conditions that Shylock must meet for these kindnesses. First, he must immediately convert and become a Christian. Second, he must sign a deed of gift here in this court, leaving all he possesses at the time of his death to his son-in-law, Lorenzo, and his daughter."

The Duke replied, "Shylock shall do these things, or else I will recant the pardon of his life that I just pronounced here."

"Does this satisfy you, Jew?" Portia asked. "What do you say?"

Shylock hesitated, thought, and then said, "I am satisfied."

Portia said, "Clerk, draw up a deed of gift."

"Please, give me permission to go from here," Shylock requested of the Duke. "I am not well. Send the deed of gift to me after it has been drawn up, and I will sign it."

"You may leave," the Duke said, "but be sure to sign the deed of gift."

Gratiano said, "You will become a Christian. In your christening, you will have two godfathers. Had I been judge, you would have had ten more. Twelve people make up a jury, and they would have found you guilty and sent you to the gallows, not to the christening font."

His heart heavy, Shylock departed. At home, he may have realized that he was morally wrong to insist on receiving a pound of Antonio's flesh.

The Duke said to Portia, "Sir, I ask you to come home with me and eat dinner."

"I humbly ask your grace to pardon me," Portia replied, "because I cannot. I must return to Padua this night, and I need to immediately set forth."

"I am sorry that you do not have the leisure to stay here for a while," the Duke said to her.

He added, "Antonio, reward this gentleman, for, in my opinion, you are much bound to him."

The Duke and the Magnificoes left the courtroom.

Bassanio said to Portia, "Most worthy gentleman, because of your wisdom my friend and I have been this day relieved from paying some grievous penalties. Because of that, these three thousand ducats, which were owed to the Jew, we freely give to you for your courteous pains on our behalf."

Antonio said, "We stand indebted to you, over and above this gift of three thousand ducats. We owe you our respect and friendship and service for evermore."

"He is well paid who is well satisfied," Portia said. "And I, having delivered you from grievous penalties, am well satisfied and on that account I consider myself to be well paid. My mind has so far never been interested in money. Please, know me when we meet again. I wish you well, and so I take my leave."

Portia thought, *I certainly hope that Bassanio will recognize me when we meet again — and that he will know me in the Biblical sense.*

Bassanio said to Portia, "Dear sir, it is necessary that I try harder to thank you. Take some remembrance from us — Antonio and me — as a tribute, not as a fee. Please grant me two things. First, do not deny my request, and second, pardon me for pressing you to do this."

"You are pressing me to accept remembrances from you two," Portia said, "and therefore I will yield."

To Antonio, she said, "Give me your gloves. I'll wear them in remembrance of you."

Antonio took off his gloves and gave them to Portia.

Portia thought, *I remember what Bassanio, my husband, said about me earlier: "Antonio, I am married to a wife who is as dear to me as life itself, but life itself, my wife, and all the world are not by me esteemed above your life. I would lose all — yes, I would sacrifice my life, my wife, and all the world — to this Devil, to deliver you from him and so save your life." I will tease him later because of what he said just now.*

She said to Bassanio, "And, out of respect for you and your request of me, I'll take this ring from you."

Bassanio drew back his hand. He thought, *This is the ring that my wife gave to me. Portia told me, "I give you this ring; if you ever part from, lose, or give away this ring, let it foretell the ruin and decay of your love and be my opportunity to denounce you." I told her, "When this ring that you have given me parts from this finger, then life will part from me. When I no longer wear this ring, then you may say boldly that I, Bassanio, am dead."*

Portia said to him, "Do not draw back your hand; I'll take no more than this ring. Out of respect for me, you shall not deny me this."

Bassanio said, "This ring, good sir, it is a trifle! I will not shame myself by giving you this."

"I will have nothing else except only this," Portia said. "Now that I think about it, I like this ring and I really want it."

"This ring has more value than merely monetary value," Bassanio said. "Allow me to give you instead of it the most monetarily valuable ring in all of Venice. I will find the most monetarily valuable ring by having announcements made in public. Allow me to give you that ring rather than this ring, please."

Portia told him, "I see, sir, that you are liberal in making offers of gifts, but not in actually giving gifts. You taught me first to beg, and now I think that you are teaching me how a beggar should be answered. Beggars cannot be choosers; they must take what they are given."

"Good sir, this ring was given to me by my wife, and when she put it on me, she made me vow that I should not sell it or give it away or lose it," Bassanio said.

"That excuse helps many men keep the 'gifts' that they have promised to give," Portia said, "If your wife is not a madwoman, and if she knows how well I have deserved the ring, she would not be your enemy forever just because you gave it to me. Well, may peace be with you!"

Portia and Nerissa left the courtroom.

Antonio, who owed Portia his life and who did not know the marital and emotional value of the ring, said, "My Lord Bassanio, let him have the ring. Let his deserving conduct and my friendship be valued against your wife's commandment."

Bassanio decided to give the young doctor of law his ring. He took it off and handed it to Gratiano and said, "Go, Gratiano, run and overtake him. Give him the ring, and bring him, if you can, to Antonio's house: Go! Hurry!"

Gratiano departed, running.

Bassanio then said to Antonio, "Come, you and I will go to your house now, and early in the morning we will both journey quickly to Belmont and see my wife, Portia. Let's go now, Antonio."

On a street outside the courtroom, Portia said to Nerissa, "Ask and find out where the Jew's house is. Give him this deed of gift and have him sign it. We will leave tonight and be home in Belmont a day before our husbands get home. This deed of gift will be very welcome to Lorenzo."

Gratiano came running up to them and said to Portia, "Fair sir, I am glad that I have caught up to you. My Lord Bassanio upon further consideration has sent me to give you this ring, and he invites you to eat with him at Antonio's house."

"I cannot eat dinner with him," Portia said, "but I do accept this ring with great thanks. Please tell him that. Also, please show my young clerk where old Shylock's house is."

"I will do that," Gratiano said.

Nerissa said to Portia, "Sir, I would like to speak with you for a moment privately."

Nerissa thought, *In the courtroom, my husband, Gratiano, said, "I have a wife, whom I love, but I wish that she were dead and in Heaven, so she could entreat some Heavenly power to change the mind of this currish Jew." I will tease him later because of what he said just now.*

Nerissa and Portia went a short distance from Gratiano, and Nerissa whispered, "I'll see if I can get my husband's ring, the one that I made him swear to keep forever."

Portia whispered, "I am sure that you can get it from him. Our husbands will later swear to us mightily that they gave the rings away to men, but we will boldly contradict them and say that they gave the rings away to women — which will be true — and we will outswear them, too."

Portia said out loud, "Go now! Make haste. You know where you can meet me later."

Nerissa said to Gratiano, "Come, good sir, and show me the way to the Jew's house."

CHAPTER 5

— 5.1 —

On the avenue leading to Portia's house, Lorenzo and Jessica were playfully talking together. They were competing in a game in which they talked about love matches that ended badly. Although they seemed to be lighthearted, they were worried. Jessica had stolen much wealth from Shylock, her father, but she and Lorenzo had squandered much — or all — of it. Possibly, they were thinking that they would act more responsibly if they could replay their recent actions.

Lorenzo said, "The moon shines brightly. On such a night as this, when the sweet wind gently kissed the trees and they made no noise, on such a night as this I think that Troilus mounted the Trojan walls and sighed his soul toward the Grecian tents, where Cressida, the woman he loved, lay that night."

Cressida became unfaithful to Troilus.

"On such a night as this, did Thisbe fearfully walk on the dewy grass and saw the lion's shadow before she saw the lion and ran away, dismayed," Jessica said.

Thisbe dropped her mantle — her shawl — as she fled from the lion, which tore it. Her lover, Pyramus, found the mantle, thought that the lion had devoured Thisbe, and killed himself. Thisbe found his body, and she killed herself.

"On such a night as this, Dido stood with a willow branch — a symbol of unrequited love — in her hand upon the shore of the wild sea and beckoned her lover to return to Carthage," Lorenzo said.

Aeneas had left Dido, Queen of Carthage, in order to go to Italy and become an important ancestor of the Roman people, as was his destiny. Dido cursed Aeneas' descendants and then committed suicide.

"On such a night as this, Medea gathered the enchanted herbs that made old Aeson young again," Jessica said.

Aeson was the father of Jason, whom Medea had married. Jason later was unfaithful to Medea, who murdered the children whom they had had together.

"On such a night as this, Jessica stole wealth from and stole away from her father the wealthy Jew and with a spendthrift lover ran away from Venice as far as Belmont," Lorenzo said.

"On such a night as this, young Lorenzo swore that he loved Jessica. He stole her soul with many vows of faith, not one vow of which was true," Jessica said.

"On such a night as this, pretty Jessica, like a little shrew, slandered her lover, and he forgave her," Lorenzo said.

Jessica said, "I would outdo you in mentioning nights if no one would interrupt us, but I hear a man's footsteps coming toward us."

Stephano, one of Portia's servants, walked up to them.

"Who is walking so fast in the silence of the night?" Lorenzo asked.

"A friend," Stephano replied.

"A friend! What friend? What is your name, please, friend?" Lorenzo asked.

"Stephano is my name, and I bring you word that Portia, my mistress, will before the break of day arrive here at Belmont. She has been going to roadside shrines where by holy crosses she kneels and prays for a happy marriage."

"Who is coming with her?" Lorenzo asked.

"No one except a holy hermit and Nerissa, her waiting-gentlewoman. Please tell me, has my master, Bassanio, returned yet?"

"He has not, nor have we received any message from him," Lorenzo replied.

He added, "Jessica, let us go inside, please, and prepare a ceremony of welcome for Portia, the mistress of the house."

Launcelot the fool appeared. Pretending not to find Lorenzo, for whom he was searching, he called "Sola! Sola! Wo ha, ho! Sola! Sola!"

"Wo ha, ho!" is a hunting cry. "Sola!" is both a hunting cry and an imitation of the sound of a post horn. Launcelot was hunting for Lorenzo to tell him that a post — an express messenger — had arrived with news for him.

"Who is shouting?" Lorenzo shouted.

"Sola!" Launcelot shouted. "Have you seen Master Lorenzo? Master Lorenzo, sola! Sola!"

"Stop shouting," Lorenzo ordered. "I am here."

"Sola!" Launcelot shouted. "Where are you?"

"Here I am."

Pretending that Lorenzo was not Lorenzo, Launcelot said, "Tell him that a post has come from my master, with his horn full of good news — a cornucopia of good news. That good news is that my master will be here before morning."

Lorenzo said to Jessica, "Sweet soul, let's go inside, and there we will await their coming. And yet we need not go in. My friend Stephano, tell everyone in the house, please, that your mistress is at hand. Have Portia's musicians come outside so that they can welcome her with music."

Stephano went inside the house.

Lorenzo said to Jessica, "How sweet the moonlight sleeps upon this bank! Here will we sit and let the sounds of music creep into our ears. Soft stillness and the night well suit the touches of musicians' hands on instruments of sweet harmony.

"Sit, Jessica. Look how the floor of Heaven is thickly inlaid with tiles of bright gold — planets and stars. There is not the smallest orb that you see but sings in his motion like an angel. The planets and stars produce the music of the spheres and always sing like a choir to the young-eyed angels known as the cherubim. Such harmony is in immortal souls, but while our souls are trapped in this muddy vesture of decay — this mortal human body that grossly encloses our immortal soul — we cannot hear it."

The musicians came out of Portia's house.

Lorenzo said to them, "Come, and wake Diana with a hymn! Diana the Moon goddess is sleeping behind clouds. With your sweetest touches on your musical instruments, wake Diana and draw her out from behind the clouds with music. And with your music, guide your mistress to her home."

Jessica said, "I am never merry when I hear sweet music. Music puts me in a contemplative and reflective mood."

Lorenzo replied, "The reason for that is your soul is attentive to the music. We have seen a wild and wanton herd of youthful and untrained colts racing around and making mad jumps, bellowing and neighing loudly. That is the hot nature of their excited spirit; however, if they by chance hear the sound of a trumpet, or if any other air of music touches their ears, you shall see them standing still together. Their savage eyes adopt a modest gaze because of the sweet power of music. That is the basis of truth that the poet Ovid exaggerated when he wrote that the musician Orpheus was able to make trees, stones, and floods come to him when he played.

"There is nothing so stubborn, hard, and full of rage that music, while it plays, cannot change that thing's nature. The man who does not like music and is not moved by the concord of sweet sounds, is fit for treasons, plots and deeds of great violence, and destruction and acts of pillage. The impulses of his mind are as cheerless and gloomy as night and his affections are as dark as Erebus, that region of darkness in the afterlife. Let no such man be trusted. Listen to the music."

Portia and Nerissa arrived.

Portia said to Nerissa, "That light we see is burning in my hall. How far that little candle throws its beams! So shines a good deed in an evil world."

"When the Moon shone before it went behind a cloud, we did not see the candle," Nerissa replied.

"The greater glory dims the lesser glory," Portia said. "The representative of a King shines as brightly as the King until the King arrives, and then the representative of the King loses his glory. His glory vanishes the way that an inland brook flows into and vanishes into the ocean. Listen, I hear music!"

"The musicians of your house are playing," Nerissa said.

"Nothing is good, I see, without the right context. I think that their music sounds much sweeter now than it does in the daytime."

"The silence of the night makes the music sound much better, madam," Nerissa said.

"The crow sings as sweetly as the lark, when no one is listening to their songs," Portia said. "I think that the nightingale, which sings at night, if she should sing by day, when every goose is cackling, would be thought to be no better a singer than the wren. How many things are well seasoned when they occur at the proper season! When they occur at exactly the right time, their flavor is so much better and they enjoy rightful praise because they are true perfection!"

The Moon was still behind the clouds, and Portia called to the musicians, "Quiet! The Moon goddess Diana is sleeping beside her loved one, Endymion, and would not be awakened."

The music stopped, and Lorenzo said, "That is the voice, unless I am much deceived, of Portia."

Portia said, "He knows that it is I the same way that the blind man knows the presence of the cuckoo — by the bad voice."

"Dear lady, welcome home," Lorenzo said.

Portia said to him, "Nerissa and I have been praying for our husbands' welfare. We hope that our husbands will prosper all the better for our words.

"Have they returned?"

"Madam, they are not yet here," Lorenzo replied, "but a messenger arrived not long ago to tell us that they are coming soon."

"Go inside, Nerissa," Portia said. "Tell my servants that they are not to mention to our husbands that we have been absent from home. Lorenzo, and you, too, Jessica, do not tell our husbands that we have been away."

Nerissa went inside.

A distinctive trumpet call sounded to announce that Bassanio was coming.

Lorenzo said, "Your husband is near at hand. I hear his trumpet call. We are no tattletales, madam; don't be afraid that we will let your husbands know that you have been absent."

Portia started to talk about the weather so that her husband would not suspect that she had just been talking about him — and about keeping something secret from him.

"This night, I think, is like ill daylight. It looks a little paler. It is like a very cloudy day during which the Sun remains hidden."

Bassanio, Antonio, Gratiano, and their servants arrived.

Bassanio, who had overheard Portia's last comment, said to her, "If you would walk outside at night when the Sun is hidden, we would enjoy sunlight at the same time as do the people who live on the other side of the Earth."

"Let me give light, but let me not be light," Portia said. "A wife with light heels raises them high in the air and parts them so she can be promiscuous. Such a light wife makes a husband heavy-hearted and full of sorrow, and I never want Bassanio to feel that way because of me. But let everything be as God wishes it to be! You are welcome home, my lord."

Gratiano went inside the house to look for his wife.

"I thank you, madam," Bassanio replied. "Welcome my friend. This is the man — this is Antonio — to whom I am so infinitely bound."

"You should in all senses be much bound to him," Portia said, "because I hear that he was much bound — in the chains of a prisoner — for you."

Antonio said, "I have been freed from those chains and amply repaid for my distress by the friendship of your husband."

Portia replied, "Sir, you are very welcome to our house. I intend to show you that by my actions, and therefore I will not waste time with pretty words."

Gratiano and Jessica came out from inside the house. They were talking about Jessica's ring, the one that Gratiano had given to the clerk of the young lawyer who had served as the judge in the trial of Antonio.

Gratiano said to Jessica, "By yonder Moon, I swear that you do me wrong. Truly, I gave your ring to the lawyer's clerk. I wish that the clerk would be castrated since you, my love, are taking the loss of your ring so much to heart."

"A quarrel?" Portia said. "Already! You haven't even celebrated your wedding night! What's the matter?"

"We are talking about a hoop of gold," Gratiano said, "a little ring that she gave me that had a motto inscribed inside that was like one of the verses that are inscribed on the handles of knives. It said, '*Love me, and leave me not.*'"

Nerissa said, "Why are you talking about the motto and the littleness of the ring? You swore to me, when I gave the ring to you, that you would wear it until the hour you died and that it should lie with you in your grave. Even if you did not keep the ring out of respect for me, yet because of your vehement oaths you ought to have been careful and kept it. You said that you gave my ring to a judge's clerk! As God is my judge, the clerk you gave the ring to will never grow hair on his face!"

Gratiano said, "He will, if he lives long enough to become a man."

Nerissa replied, "That is true — if a woman lives long enough to become a man."

Gratiano said, "Now, I swear by my hand that I gave it to a youth, a boy, a diminutive and very clean boy, no taller than yourself, the judge's clerk, a chattering boy who begged it as a fee. I could not in my heart deny giving it to him.'"

"You are to blame," Portia said. "I must be plain with you. You parted very lightly and easily with your wife's first gift to you: a ring that you, with oaths, put on your finger. Therefore, the ring became riveted to your body by your oaths. I gave my love, Bassanio, a ring and made him swear never to part with it; and here he stands. I dare be sworn for him that he would not part from the ring or pluck it from his finger for all the wealth that is the world. Now, truly, Gratiano, you have unkindly given your wife a reason to grieve. If that had happened to me, I would be very angry because of it."

Bassanio, who had also given away his ring, thought, *The best thing for me to do is to cut off my left hand and swear that I lost my hand as I fought to keep the ring.*

Gratiano was no help to him: "My Lord Bassanio gave his ring away to the young judge who begged for it and indeed deserved it, too, and then the boy, his clerk, who took some pains in writing, begged for my ring, and neither the young judge nor his boy would accept anything other than the rings."

"Which ring did you give to the judge, Bassanio?" Portia asked. "Not that ring, I hope, that I gave to you."

"If a lie could help me out here, I would lie," Bassanio replied, "but you can see that my finger does not have your ring on it. The ring is gone."

"And truth has departed from your false heart," Portia said. "By Heaven, I will never sleep with you until I see the ring I gave you."

Nerissa said to Gratiano, "And I will never sleep with you until I see the ring I gave you."

"Sweet Portia," Bassanio said, "if you knew to whom I gave the ring, if you knew for whom I gave the ring, if you knew why I gave the ring and if you knew how unwillingly I left behind the ring, when nothing would be accepted except the ring, you would not be so displeased."

Portia replied, using the same form of language as her husband, "If you had known the special quality of the ring, if you had known half the worthiness of the woman who gave you the ring, and if you had known how much your own honor depended on keeping the ring, you would never have parted with the ring. What man exists who is so unreasonable — if you had been willing to have defended the ring with any zeal — that he would have lacked the courtesy to allow you to keep the ring because of its marital, emotional value? Nerissa teaches me what I should believe: She believes that Gratiano gave her ring to a woman, and I believe the same thing about you and my ring. I bet my life that you gave my ring to a woman."

"No, by my honor, Portia, and by my soul," Bassanio said, "no woman got your ring. I gave it to a doctor of civil law who refused to accept three thousand ducats from me and instead begged for the ring, which I would not give to him. I allowed him to go away displeased although he had saved the life of my very dear friend. What should I say, sweet lady? I had to send the ring to him; I was overcome by shame, and my courtesy and honor would not allow ingratitude to so besmear my name. Pardon me, good lady, for, by these blessed candles of the night — the stars — had you been there, I think you would have begged from me your ring so that you could give it to the worthy doctor."

Bassanio was courteous. He did not mention Antonio, who had urged him to give the ring to the young doctor of civil law.

"Allow that doctor to never come near my house," Portia said. "Since he has gotten the ring that I loved, and which you swore to keep, I will become as liberal — licentious, in fact — as you. I will not deny him anything I have — no, I will not deny the possession of my body or my husband's bed. Know him I shall, I am sure of it. Do not sleep even one night away from home; watch me like Argus, the monster with the hundred eyes. If you do not watch me continually, if I am left alone, I swear, by my honor, which is still my own, I will have that doctor as my bedfellow."

Nerissa said, "And I will have that doctor's clerk as my bedfellow. Therefore, think carefully about whether you ever want to leave me alone."

"Well, if you do take him as your bedfellow," Gratiano said, "never let me catch him because if I do I will break his pen — and I will break his male appendage that can be compared to a pen."

"I am the unhappy cause of these quarrels," Antonio said.

"Sir, do not grieve," Portia said to him. "You are welcome nevertheless."

"Portia, forgive me this wrong I was forced to do," Bassanio said, "and with these my many friends as witnesses, I swear to you by your own beautiful eyes, in which I see myself — "

Portia interrupted, "Did everyone hear that! In my eyes he doubly sees himself. In each of my eyes, he sees a reflection of his face. Swear by your double self, my two-faced husband — that is an oath that will do you credit."

"Please hear me out," Bassanio said. "Pardon this fault, and by my soul I swear that I never more will break an oath that I have made to you."

Antonio said, "I once did lend my body as surety for him to be able to gain wealth. This would have gone badly wrong except for the young doctor who now has the ring that you gave to your husband. I dare to lend myself again as surety. This time, I will lend my immortal soul, which is much more valuable than my mortal body. I will lend my immortal soul as surety that your lord will never again knowingly break an oath that he has made to you."

"Then you shall be his surety," Portia said.

She gave him her ring and said to Antonio, "Give this ring to my husband and tell him to take better care of it than he did the other ring."

"Here, Lord Bassanio," Antonio said. "Swear to keep this ring safe."

"By Heaven," Bassanio said, "this is the same ring that I gave to the doctor of civil law!"

"I got this ring from him," Portia said. "Pardon me, Bassanio, for I swear by this ring that the doctor lay with me."

Nerissa said, "And pardon me, my gentle Gratiano, because that same diminutive, very clean boy, the doctor's clerk, did lie with me last night and gave me this ring."

She handed him the ring that he had given away.

Gratiano said, "Why, this is similar to the mending of roads in the summer, when they do not need to be mended. You women have no need to seek lovers because your husbands are still young and vigorous. What, have we been made cuckolds before we have deserved it?"

"Don't be gross," Portia said. "You are all amazed and bewildered, but we can explain everything. Here is a letter; read it at your leisure. It comes from Padua, from Bellario. In this letter, you will learn that I, Portia, was the doctor of civil law and that Nerissa was my clerk: Lorenzo here will testify that we set forth as soon as you left and have just now returned — I have not yet entered my house. Antonio, you are welcome here, and I have better news in store for you than you expect. Unseal and read this letter; you shall find in it the news that three of your merchant ships, richly loaded, have come into harbor safely and suddenly. I will not tell you how I happen to have this letter."

"I am astonished; I cannot speak," Antonio said. He opened and began to read the letter.

"Were you really the doctor of civil law?" Bassanio asked. Did I really not recognize you?"

Gratiano asked Nerissa, "Were you really the clerk who is going to make me a cuckold?"

"Yes, but I can say that the clerk will never make you a cuckold unless he lives long enough to become a man."

"Sweet doctor, you shall be my bedfellow," Bassanio said to Portia. "Whenever I am absent, then I give you permission to sleep with my wife."

Having finished reading the letter, Antonio said, "Sweet lady, you saved my life and now you have given me the news that I will have the money that I need to live. In this letter, I read for certain that my ships have safely come into harbor."

"And now, Lorenzo," Portia said, "my clerk has some good news for you, too."

"That is true," Nerissa said, "and I will freely give him the good news. Here I give to you and Jessica, from the rich Jew, a special deed of gift. After his death, all that he dies possessed of, Shylock leaves to you."

"Fair ladies, you drop manna in front of starved people," said Lorenzo, the spendthrift — or, perhaps, former spendthrift.

"It is almost morning," Portia said, "and yet I am sure you are not fully satisfied with our accounts of these events. You still have questions to ask Nerissa and me. Let us go inside, and there you can interrogate us on oath. And we will faithfully and truthfully answer all questions."

"Let us do that," Gratiano said, "and the first question that I will ask my wife, Nerissa, is whether she would rather wait until the coming night to go to bed and consummate our marriage, or go to bed now, with two hours remaining until the break of day. But if she wants to wait, throughout the coming day I will wish that it were dark so that I could go to bed and sleep with the doctor's clerk. Well, as long as I live I'll worry about nothing as much as keeping safe Nerissa's ring."

He thought, *Wedding rings are symbols. A finger goes into the ring. The finger is a phallic symbol, and the ring is a symbol of a feminine circle. I plan on taking care of Nerissa's ring — and of her circle.*

NOTA BENE

1) The merchant of Venice is Antonio; the Jew of Venice is Shylock.

2) In the Middle Ages and the Renaissance, Jews were often moneylenders because Christians believed that lending money at interest was a sin. Usury then meant lending money at interest; it now means lending money at an excessively high rate of interest. Christians no longer believe that lending money and charging interest is necessarily a sin. Indeed, it is an important part of modern economies.

Lending at interest may be permissible in certain instances; certainly we capitalist Americans believe that. I personally see lots of good reasons for lending at interest. Bonds raise money for investments. However, at times lending at interest is not ethical. For example, the lending could be done at excessively high rates of interest. Here I think of the check-cashing places that prey on the poor. The people who own the check-cashing places can end up in Hell.

However, although we Americans may believe in lending at interest, the Bible may prohibit it — at least in certain cases. For example, thou shalt not lend money at interest to your brother, especially if your brother is poor, although you may lend money at interest to strangers. Here are a few Bible passages about lending at interest:

Deuteronomy 23:19: *Thou shalt not lend upon usury to thy brother; usury of money, usury of victuals, usury of any thing that is lent upon usury:*

Exodus 22:25: *If thou lend money to any of my people that is poor by thee, thou shalt not be to him as an usurer, neither shalt thou lay upon him usury.*

Leviticus 25:35-37: *And if thy brother be waxen poor, and fallen in decay with thee; then thou shalt relieve him: yea, though he be a stranger, or a sojourner; that he may live with thee. Take thou no usury of him, or increase: but fear thy God; that thy brother may live with thee. Thou shalt not give him thy money upon usury, nor lend him thy victuals for increase.*

Deuteronomy 23:20: *Unto a stranger thou mayest lend upon usury; but unto thy brother thou shalt not lend upon usury: that the LORD thy God may bless thee in all that thou settest thine hand to in the land whither thou goest to possess it.*

Has Shylock violated any of these commandments?

3) We really do see a lot of prejudice in this play. Portia prefers to marry someone with a light skin, and Antonio hates Jews. Portia happily marries Bassanio, and Bassanio happily marries her, but an impartial observer could very well say that Bassanio is marrying Portia for her money. The Prince of Morocco, although he is proud, has many more accomplishments than Bassanio. However, mercy is a theme of the play. We can ask why Portia would not want to marry the Prince of Morocco. If she were to marry him, she would have to move to his home in his country. By marrying Bassanio, she can probably stay in her home in Belmont. A person with a dark skin who has status high enough to marry Portia is most likely someone who lives in a country other than her own.

4) One theme of the play is the harmful effects that prejudice can have on people. It can make someone want to cut a pound of flesh from a living person. It can make someone spit on the clothing and the beard of an old man and kick him.

5) We sympathize with Shylock because he is the victim of prejudice, but he also is guilty of prejudice. He hates Antonio in part because he is a Christian, although he has some other very good reasons for hating Antonio. We ought not to sympathize with Shylock when he wants Antonio to pay the penalty that is in the contract that Antonio signed. Being the victim of prejudice can help cause someone to be prejudiced; prejudice creates more prejudice.

6) Many Christians of the time that the play is set believed that the only way to get to Heaven was through believing in Jesus Christ and therefore Jews would be damned to Hell. Because of this belief, they would regard the conversion of a Jew to Christianity — even a forced conversion — to be a good thing. Here is an important Bible verse for understanding this belief:

John 14:6: *Jesus saith unto him, I am the way, the truth, and the life: no man cometh unto the Father, but by me.*

If we were to be merciful when judging Antonio, we might think that he wants to save Shylock's soul. Of course, most people today think that a forced confession is contemptible and worthless.

Antonio does show concern for Lorenzo and Jessica's financial security. He wants to make sure that Shylock provides for them after Shylock's death; thus, he forces Shylock to sign the deed of gift.

Is it possible that Antonio is also concerned about Shylock's financial security? Near the end of the play, he wishes to take half of Shylock's wealth and invest it. No doubt that money would be invested in Antonio's trade with other countries. Does Antonio intend to give the profit made by Shylock's money to Shylock? Possibly. Shylock cannot make money by lending at interest since he will convert to Christianity, and so he has no way to make a living. Antonio may intend to make sure that Shylock has money on which to live. Certainly, at the end of the play, three of Antonio's ships, richly loaded, have returned safely to the harbor of Venice, and so Antonio now has enough money to live on. Of course, we need to remember that Antonio has called Shylock names and spit on him and kicked him. Also, of course, Shylock was prepared to cut off a pound of flesh from Antonio's living body. Antonio may have wanted half of Shylock's wealth simply because at the time Antonio desperately needed money.

Appendix A: About the Author

It was a dark and stormy night. Suddenly a cry rang out, and on a hot summer night in 1954, Josephine, wife of Carl Bruce, gave birth to a boy — me. Unfortunately, this young married couple allowed Reuben Saturday, Josephine's brother, to name their first-born. Reuben, aka "The Joker," decided that Bruce was a nice name, so he decided to name me Bruce Bruce. I have gone by my middle name — David — ever since.

Being named Bruce David Bruce hasn't been all bad. Bank tellers remember me very quickly, so I don't often have to show an ID. It can be fun in charades, also. When I was a counselor as a teenager at Camp Echoing Hills in Warsaw, Ohio, a fellow counselor gave the signs for "sounds like" and "two words," then she pointed to a bruise on her leg twice. Bruise Bruise? Oh yeah, Bruce Bruce is the answer!

Uncle Reuben, by the way, gave me a haircut when I was in kindergarten. He cut my hair short and shaved a small bald spot on the back of my head. My mother wouldn't let me go to school until the bald spot grew out again.

Of all my brothers and sisters (six in all), I am the only transplant to Athens, Ohio. I was born in Newark, Ohio, and have lived all around Southeastern Ohio. However, I moved to Athens to go to Ohio University and have never left.

At Ohio U, I never could make up my mind whether to major in English or Philosophy, so I got a bachelor's degree with a double major in both areas, then I added a master's degree in English and a master's degree in Philosophy.

Currently, and for a long time to come (I eat fruits and veggies), I am spending my retirement writing books such as *Nadia Comaneci: Perfect 10*, *The Funniest People in Dance*, *Homer's* Iliad: *A Retelling in Prose*, and *William Shakespeare's* Othello: *A Retelling in Prose*.

By the way, my sister Brenda Kennedy writes romances such as *A New Beginning* and *Shattered Dreams*.

Appendix B: Some Books by David Bruce

Retellings of a Classic Work of Literature

Arden of Faversham: *A Retelling*

Ben Jonson's The Alchemist: *A Retelling*

Ben Jonson's The Arraignment, or Poetaster: *A Retelling*

Ben Jonson's Bartholomew Fair: *A Retelling*

Ben Jonson's The Case is Altered: *A Retelling*

Ben Jonson's Catiline's Conspiracy: *A Retelling*

Ben Jonson's The Devil is an Ass: *A Retelling*

Ben Jonson's Epicene: *A Retelling*

Ben Jonson's Every Man in His Humor: *A Retelling*

Ben Jonson's Every Man Out of His Humor: *A Retelling*

Ben Jonson's The Fountain of Self-Love, or Cynthia's Revels: *A Retelling*

Ben Jonson's The Magnetic Lady, or Humors Reconciled: *A Retelling*

Ben Jonson's The New Inn, or The Light Heart: *A Retelling*

Ben Jonson's Sejanus' Fall: *A Retelling*

Ben Jonson's The Staple of News: *A Retelling*

Ben Jonson's A Tale of a Tub: *A Retelling*

Ben Jonson's Volpone, or the Fox: *A Retelling*

Christopher Marlowe's Complete Plays: Retellings

Christopher Marlowe's Dido, Queen of Carthage: *A Retelling*

Christopher Marlowe's Doctor Faustus: *Retellings of the 1604 A-Text and of the 1616 B-Text*

Christopher Marlowe's Edward II: *A Retelling*

Christopher Marlowe's The Massacre at Paris: *A Retelling*

Christopher Marlowe's The Rich Jew of Malta: *A Retelling*

Christopher Marlowe's Tamburlaine, Parts 1 and 2: *Retellings*

Dante's Divine Comedy: *A Retelling in Prose*

Dante's Inferno: *A Retelling in Prose*

Dante's Purgatory: *A Retelling in Prose*

Dante's Paradise: *A Retelling in Prose*

The Famous Victories of Henry V: *A Retelling*

From the Iliad *to the* Odyssey: *A Retelling in Prose of Quintus of Smyrna's* Posthomerica

George Chapman, Ben Jonson, and John Marston's Eastward Ho! *A Retelling*

George Peele's The Arraignment of Paris: *A Retelling*

George Peele's The Battle of Alcazar: *A Retelling*

George's Peele's David and Bathsheba, and the Tragedy of Absalom: *A Retelling*

George Peele's Edward I: *A Retelling*

George Peele's The Old Wives' Tale: *A Retelling*

George-a-Greene: *A Retelling*

The History of King Leir: *A Retelling*
Homer's Iliad: *A Retelling in Prose*
Homer's Odyssey: *A Retelling in Prose*
J.W. Gent.'s The Valiant Scot: *A Retelling*
Jason and the Argonauts: A Retelling in Prose of Apollonius of Rhodes' Argonautica
John Ford: Eight Plays Translated into Modern English
John Ford's The Broken Heart: *A Retelling*
John Ford's The Fancies, Chaste and Noble: *A Retelling*
John Ford's The Lady's Trial: *A Retelling*
John Ford's The Lover's Melancholy: *A Retelling*
John Ford's Love's Sacrifice: *A Retelling*
John Ford's Perkin Warbeck: *A Retelling*
John Ford's The Queen: *A Retelling*
John Ford's 'Tis Pity She's a Whore: *A Retelling*
John Lyly's Campaspe: *A Retelling*
John Lyly's Endymion, The Man in the Moon: *A Retelling*
John Lyly's Galatea: *A Retelling*
John Lyly's Love's Metamorphosis: *A Retelling*
John Lyly's Midas: *A Retelling*
John Lyly's Mother Bombie: *A Retelling*
John Lyly's Sappho and Phao: *A Retelling*
John Lyly's The Woman in the Moon: *A Retelling*
John Webster's The White Devil: *A Retelling*
King Edward III: *A Retelling*
Mankind: *A Medieval Morality Play* (A Retelling)
Margaret Cavendish's The Unnatural Tragedy: *A Retelling*
The Merry Devil of Edmonton: *A Retelling*
The Summoning of Everyman: *A Medieval Morality Play* (A Retelling)
Robert Greene's Friar Bacon and Friar Bungay: *A Retelling*
The Taming of a Shrew: *A Retelling*
Tarlton's Jests: A Retelling
Thomas Middleton's A Chaste Maid in Cheapside: *A Retelling*
Thomas Middleton's Women Beware Women: *A Retelling*
Thomas Middleton and Thomas Dekker's The Roaring Girl: *A Retelling*
Thomas Middleton and William Rowley's The Changeling: *A Retelling*
The Trojan War and Its Aftermath: Four Ancient Epic Poems
Virgil's Aeneid: *A Retelling in Prose*
William Shakespeare's 5 Late Romances: Retellings in Prose
William Shakespeare's 10 Histories: Retellings in Prose
William Shakespeare's 11 Tragedies: Retellings in Prose
William Shakespeare's 12 Comedies: Retellings in Prose
William Shakespeare's 38 Plays: Retellings in Prose

William Shakespeare's 1 Henry IV, aka Henry IV, Part 1: *A Retelling in Prose*

William Shakespeare's 2 Henry IV, aka Henry IV, Part 2: *A Retelling in Prose*

William Shakespeare's 1 Henry VI, aka Henry VI, Part 1: *A Retelling in Prose*

William Shakespeare's 2 Henry VI, aka Henry VI, Part 2: *A Retelling in Prose*

William Shakespeare's 3 Henry VI, aka Henry VI, Part 3: *A Retelling in Prose*

William Shakespeare's All's Well that Ends Well: *A Retelling in Prose*

William Shakespeare's Antony and Cleopatra: *A Retelling in Prose*

William Shakespeare's As You Like It: *A Retelling in Prose*

William Shakespeare's The Comedy of Errors: *A Retelling in Prose*

William Shakespeare's Coriolanus: *A Retelling in Prose*

William Shakespeare's Cymbeline: *A Retelling in Prose*

William Shakespeare's Hamlet: *A Retelling in Prose*

William Shakespeare's Henry V: *A Retelling in Prose*

William Shakespeare's Henry VIII: *A Retelling in Prose*

William Shakespeare's Julius Caesar: *A Retelling in Prose*

William Shakespeare's King John: *A Retelling in Prose*

William Shakespeare's King Lear: *A Retelling in Prose*

William Shakespeare's Love's Labor's Lost: *A Retelling in Prose*

William Shakespeare's Macbeth: *A Retelling in Prose*

William Shakespeare's Measure for Measure: *A Retelling in Prose*

William Shakespeare's The Merchant of Venice: *A Retelling in Prose*

William Shakespeare's The Merry Wives of Windsor: *A Retelling in Prose*

William Shakespeare's A Midsummer Night's Dream: *A Retelling in Prose*

William Shakespeare's Much Ado About Nothing: *A Retelling in Prose*

William Shakespeare's Othello: *A Retelling in Prose*

William Shakespeare's Pericles, Prince of Tyre: *A Retelling in Prose*

William Shakespeare's Richard II: *A Retelling in Prose*

William Shakespeare's Richard III: *A Retelling in Prose*

William Shakespeare's Romeo and Juliet: *A Retelling in Prose*

William Shakespeare's The Taming of the Shrew: *A Retelling in Prose*

William Shakespeare's The Tempest: *A Retelling in Prose*

William Shakespeare's Timon of Athens: *A Retelling in Prose*

William Shakespeare's Titus Andronicus: *A Retelling in Prose*

William Shakespeare's Troilus and Cressida: *A Retelling in Prose*

William Shakespeare's Twelfth Night: *A Retelling in Prose*

William Shakespeare's The Two Gentlemen of Verona: *A Retelling in Prose*

William Shakespeare's The Two Noble Kinsmen: *A Retelling in Prose*

William Shakespeare's The Winter's Tale: *A Retelling in Prose*